COME
AGAIN

COME AGAIN

SEX TOY EROTICA

EDITED BY
RACHEL KRAMER BUSSEL

CLEiS
PRESS

Published in the United States by Cleis Press,
an imprint of Start Midnight, LLC,
375 Hudson Street, Twelfth Floor, New York, 10014.

Printed in the United States.
Cover design: Scott Idleman/Blink
Cover photograph: Nikada/Getty Images
Text design: Frank Wiedemann

First Edition.
10 9 8 7 6 5 4 3 2 1

Trade paper ISBN: 978-1-62778-125-1
E-book ISBN: 978-1-62778-135-0

Contents

INTRODUCTION: SEX TOYS ARE EVERYWHERE

I love sex toys, both the kinds you can find in sex shops and the kinds you can find pretty much anywhere. Because the truth is, anything can become a sex toy in the right hands, and *Come Again* proves that.

In these pages, you'll read about vibrators, butt plugs, strap-on harnesses, nipple clamps, a sex doll and even a Superman dildo. But you'll also read about characters so smitten with sex toys they're willing to go to great lengths to create their own, whether it's a special bike designed to make pedaling a woman's favorite sport (in "Bikery," by Oliver Hollandaize) or an inflatable ball on a stick (as in "The Prototype," by Malin James). Perhaps in the future, we'll have sex toys like the orgasm machine being peddled in "Sex Sells," by Adriana Ravenlust, or the Simulsphere that provides "The Cure for the Common Lay," which Valerie Alexander so masterfully serves up.

Sex toys are a perfect complement to a kinky relationship, offering one person the power to control how the other uses his or her toys. In "The Secret Shopper," by Kitten Boheme, the act of shopping takes on an extremely risqué overtone, while in "Sex Kitten," by Errica Liekos, a tail and a transgression provide the perfect entrée to a hot scene.

Toys are a wonderful way for couples to double the fun, and that concept is taken to humorous and wonderful heights in "A Tale of Two Toys," by Chris Komodo, in which the popularity of remote-control vibrators is celebrated. I was awed by the way Giselle Renarde detailed the romance, wonder and pleasure a Japanese sex doll brings to a couple sharing her as they expand their sexual repertoire in "Must Love Dolls." Are Honor and Tom having a threesome with Natsuki? In their own special way, yes indeed. Dena Hankins's "Gift" shows that you're never too old to explore a new toy.

Nature lovers will appreciate the ingenuity of "Vegetable Love," by Susan St. Aubin and "Get Your Rocks Off," by Jocelyn Dex, and I know I'll be thinking about J. Crichton's "Icy Bed" every time I take out ice cubes from my freezer.

You'll find proud toy users and those whose private pleasures wind up being exposed in stories like "Dare You To," by Jillian Boyd, where the jangling of nipple clamp bells is a little too loud for comfort, and "In the Pink," by Rob Rosen, in which a masturbatory moment in the office turns into some hands-on sex education.

All of these stories celebrate sex toys for the ways they can shake up a routine, enhance an orgasm, transform an identity or simply add new delights to your sex life. Once you're done reading, I'm pretty sure, like me, you'll start seeing sex toys—or at least, potential sex toys—everywhere you go!

Rachel Kramer Bussel
Red Bank, New Jersey

DARE YOU TO

Jillian Boyd

On the one hand, I was immensely aroused, my pussy throbbing and my juices moistening my panties. On the other hand, I felt like an absolute, grade-A moron.

You would too if you'd just walked into an important presentation wearing quite possibly the noisiest pair of vibrating love balls that had ever rolled off a conveyer belt. Whoever thought they were a good idea should be fired on the spot. I whispered a little prayer that the head of Cambridge Athletics wasn't able to hear the little silicone menaces trilling about inside me, while making a mental note to give David a solid spanking for giving me this dare on this day.

It started out as the most innocent throwaway comment, made by me after I'd gotten back from a rather *interesting* night out with my brother and his mates, who were all in town for our wedding.

"Would you go out wearing a sex toy?"

David looked up from his book, his eyes peering at me from behind his glasses. "Define *going out*?"

"My brother's mate Greg just told me that he often wears a cock ring when he goes clubbing," I said, crawling into the comfortable warmth of our bed and my fiancé.

"Right. Does he know what a cock ring actually does?"

"I'm not entirely sure. He said something about always wanting to be prepared."

"What, to end up in the ER and be a water-cooler anecdote the next day?"

I chuckled, snuggling a bit closer and letting my hand slip under David's shirt. The cluster of curly chest hair was like a magnet to my fingers, but David wasn't budging from his book. Instead, he just frowned at me.

"How did you end up talking about that anyway?"

"My brother and I were discussing bachelor party favors. I suggested something cheeky, Colby said something about condoms and before I knew it, Greg and Dario were having a pretty heated debate on the best available butt plugs. It was... intriguing, let's say that."

My hand caressed David's chest, snaking its way down toward his boxers. If I could just hold his cock for a few minutes, just play with it and let off a bit of steam...but then David let out a massive yawn, which in the months leading up to this wedding had become an unfortunate code for taking a rain check on having sex.

I sighed deeply, curling myself into the duvet and consigning myself to being spooned, with a semi poking the small of my back. I hated this. All this stress about planning a nice wedding only served to make me crave intimacy with David. I wanted him to touch me, taste me, feel me...

"I like the idea of wearing a sex toy while I'm out," I eventually said, apropos of nothing.

"So you'll always be prepared?"

"No! I just like the illicitness of it. Going to work wearing a pearl thong, getting wet while you take notes on the projections for the next financial year and trying to hide your arousal. Sneaking into the bathroom at lunch with a little vibrator, getting off and then getting back to work. Fuck, just the thought of that turns me on. God knows, I need a bit of wedding-stress release."

The next evening, I came home to find a little red package on the table with a note attached to it.

> *Would you dare? Instructions inside.*
> *D x*
> *Have fun...*

I peeked. In the little red package was a black finger vibrator along with a set of instructions that made me suddenly wish I could afford to call in sick tomorrow.

The next day, at lunch, I found myself wedged into one of the ridiculously tight-spaced toilet cubes, legs spread and skirt bunched up around my waist. For such a wee vibrator, it made an almighty noise. I prayed to the God of Sex Toys that I wouldn't get caught in flagrante delicto; not only were the walls paper thin in this building, the cubicles in the women's room were also really fucking rickety.

Five minutes, David had said. I had exactly five minutes to bring myself to an orgasm, or there would be a penalty when I came home that night. So I sat back and relentlessly worked my clit with that little vibrator, until my juices were dripping down my bare thighs and I shuddered into my buzzy climax.

At five past twelve, ten minutes after I entered the room and five minutes after I took on David's dare, I texted him a picture of my postorgasmic pussy with a message: *Your turn.*

I spent the rest of the day plotting my revenge. Needless to say, when David found the little red package with the glass butt plug and the lube a few days later, he wasn't pleased.

The game was on.

"Well, thank you very much for that!" I exclaimed, wobbling back to my seat in the pub. David grinned like a shark eating overpriced cannelloni. I winced as I sat back down. I was lucky it was Monday night; there were only three other people sitting down for dinner. Thank goodness, otherwise my face would have evaporated from the blush on my cheeks.

"Did it work?"

"Of course it didn't! It's the world's smallest alley; you can't expect me to take a good picture there."

"Oh, come on, it's not that tiny."

"I was wedged between two trash cans! Not only that, but people can see into the damn place. I don't want Mr. Stevenson to see me naked, no matter how much *he'd* want to. You better not give me a penalty for this."

"Hmm…" said David, stroking his chin like an evil mastermind. "I don't know about not giving you a penalty. I mean, you didn't complete the dare, and you know our rules."

"Bloody hell, David, I nearly fell into a compost heap without any clothes on!"

"All right, all right. Let's call this off and pretend I never dared you to take a sexy naked picture in the alley next to the pub."

"Thank you. I'm getting you back for this, you know."

"I'm prepared. Bring it on. Now, come on, your pasta's getting cold."

I rolled my eyes and dug into my spaghetti. We ate in relative silence, interrupted only by more people coming in and soft music playing in the background. Then David looked up, like he'd suddenly remembered something crucial.

"I completely forgot to tell you. The florist called today. He said he wanted both of us to come in tomorrow and approve the final centerpieces."

"They're finished? I thought he said they weren't going to be ready until after the rehearsal dinner?"

David shrugged. "Apparently he's finished them. Now, if they look anywhere near what we asked him to do, I'll possibly keel over with relief."

"Well, what time does he want us there? I can't get out of work until three at the earliest."

"He said something about four thirty, so I think we're both good. It's another thing we can cross off the list, if they're actually finished."

"The never-ending list," I said, sagging back in my seat and taking a sip of my drink. "We've still got catering, cake and my final dress fitting."

David groaned. "Remind me again why we were so adamant to take all of this on ourselves?"

"Because we wanted something representative of our undying love for each other. Your words, Dave." I giggled. He stuck his tongue out at me and went on eating. My thoughts drifted, from dresses to cake to appetizers. I couldn't fathom our wedding being this close. I needed a distraction. I needed to play...

And then I had an idea.

"How do you feel about nipple clamps?"

David dropped his fork, which told me everything I needed to know. The next dare was definitely on.

KAT! YOU DIDN'T TELL ME THEY HAD
BELLS ON!
D

David's text came just as I got on the train, on the way to our appointment with the florist. The giggle I let out echoed in the carriage, leading to a couple of very weird looks from fellow passengers.

> *Oops, I forgot to tell you. They have bells on.*
> *K x*

I felt like an evil sexual mastermind. Last night, as I'd rummaged through our ever-growing stash of sex toys, I'd found the perfect pair of nipple clamps for this little dare. All David had to do was to wear them to our appointment with the florist and not get noticed.

I didn't mention the bells, specifically so I could read that reaction.

> *Jesus Kat, I'm on the Tube right now sounding like*
> *a BDSM Santa Claus. Getting looks from the tour-*
> *ists!*
> *D*

> *David, the tourists aren't going to remember you at*
> *the end of the day!*
> *Kx*

> *If I take my coat off, you can see them through my*
> *shirt!*
> *D*

*Don't take your coat off then! Besides...the thought
of you wearing those clamps is making me wet.*
Kx

Really?
D

*I'm shifting in my seat, clamping my legs together as
we speak.*
Kx

It was entirely true. The thought of David wearing nipple clamps
was enough to make me squirm and try to defuse the very potent
arousal building up in my pussy. I had to be careful—otherwise
there would be a very noticeable wet spot on my skirt.

*Is it bad that they're kind of making me a bit hard
as well?*
D

*God, I wish we weren't going to approve floral pieces
right now.*
Kx

*I could tell him to fuck off and rent a hotel room
somewhere and shag you senseless.*
D

It was a tempting idea. And as the train pulled into the station,
I stood up and felt the full brunt of the wetness that had pooled
between my thighs. God, every fiber of my being just wanted
David to push me against a wall and slide his hard, glorious

cock inside my willing opening. I'd gone way past the point of caring if anyone saw.

Nevertheless, I dutifully made my way to the florist, like a good bride-to-be, with a throbbing clit and a very wet skirt clandestinely covered by my long coat.

The bell above the shop door signaled David's arrival. His face was a cross between not-at-all pleased and impossibly aroused. He caught my eye and opened his coat to gesture to the very visible clamps under his shirt and the rather visible bulge in his work trousers. I repressed a little giggle as Nicolai the florist materialized.

"Oh good, you're both here, and on time this time. Brilliant!"

"Yes, fortunately there wasn't a major public transport delay which we had no control over this time around. I would have hated to encroach on your time, Nicolai," said David, rolling his eyes. I had to give him a little nudge, but to be fair, Nicolai had been a bit of a prick to us.

Luckily, he was a prick who couldn't detect sarcasm if it hit him in the face with a bouquet of Dutch tulips. He led us through to the back room, where our arrangements were waiting. As we walked, I repressed another giggle; I could quite clearly hear the bells on David's nipple clamps chiming as he walked. Nicolai turned around, obviously having heard something too.

"Probably just the wind. Or the bell on the door. Or both," stammered David, trying not to blush. He was fortunate to have a thick beard; otherwise he'd be as red as the roses Nicolai had used in our arrangements.

"Right. Well, as you can see here, I've tried my best to follow the brief as closely as possible. Something simple but romantic, with lots of color. I know the red roses weren't on your brief, but I saw them and I just thought they were gorgeous. I hope you don't mind."

I leaned closer toward our arrangements, gesturing to David to do the same.

"Oh, that's all right, I can see them from here," he said, knowing full well that if he leaned in, the bells would ring.

"Come on, darling. Don't you want to see the little details?"

"I can see them from here, Kat. It's perfectly fine."

But Nicolai was now tutting. "It's all right. I get a lot of men in here who can live without seeing the little finishing touches I put in."

"But you've done so much work on these. It would be a shame if David didn't see the little four-leaf clovers you put in for good luck. I like them a lot."

Nicolai beamed. "Thank you, Kat. See," he said, gesturing to David, "she is someone with an eye for detail. I like that."

Reluctantly, David gave in and leaned forward, making the bells on his clamps ring. Nicolai's head turned toward the shop entrance.

"That's strange. I swear I heard the door opening. Now, follow me into my office and we can get the final details polished and ready."

Ring-ring-ring-ring-ring. David's face was nearly on fire from embarrassment as we followed Nicolai into his office and sat down to finalize the details for the day. To make matters worse, he had the heaters on in his office.

"Oh, do take off your coats. You'll melt under all that fabric!"

I readily shrugged my coat off, not without a reminder that I still had a drying wet spot on my skirt. David brushed off Nicolai's request.

"That's all right. I'm feeling rather cold, so I'd rather keep this on."

"Nonsense! It's nice and warm in here. Take off your coat and we'll just settle the bill."

"I'd really rather not, Nicolai."

"Come on, Mr. Stone. Take off your coat. I promise we won't be long," said Nicolai, urging him along so we could settle and leave him to his work. David groaned, but slowly shed the coat, revealing his white work shirt, dotted with two little bumps around the nipple area.

Nicolai raised his eyebrows at the sight of David's protruding clamps. Fortunately for my husband-to-be, he quickly went on with the business of finalizing the details. After we settled the bill, Nicolai shook David's hand, ringing the bells yet again.

Needless to say, my future husband was utterly mortified.

His revenge, he promised, would be "sweeter than sweet." He wasn't kidding. A week after he jingled his bells at our florist appointment, I found the little red package containing the vibrating love balls. His instruction: to wear them at the presentation of my Cambridge Athletics ad campaign.

I was, quite honestly, trembling with nerves—and arousal, but mostly nerves. David knew full well that this was an important meeting that could determine the future of the advertising agency I worked for; I'd been managing this project for nearly as long as we'd been planning the wedding.

It's not a good sign when the hopes and future plans of the company rest on a woman who is desperately trying not to squirm and brush her hand against the crotch of her already soaking panties.

"Good luck today," said my boss as she entered the boardroom. "You don't need to be nervous."

"Oh, I'm not nervous, Mrs. Sedgwick, not in the slightest, not at all," I sputtered, as a particularly strong vibration coursed through my body. "I'm just trying to keep...keep my circulation up! Yes, that's why I'm all hoppy today. Got to keep fit! It's in keeping with the campaign."

"Right," she said, straightening her glasses before turning toward our clients. "Good morning, ladies and gentlemen. And welcome to Mr. Defoe from Cambridge Athletics."

As Mrs. Sedgwick spoke, I tried my best to not turn around and flash the head of Cambridge Athletics with the wet spot on my skirt. Fuck, I really should have worn something darker and less conspicuous. I braced myself and started talking, trying to keep my voice level and not squeaky from the mounting arousal.

"Cambridge Athletics is a young brand, and as you'll see, my team and I have worked very hard to KEEP in touch with the TARGET! MARKET!"

I took another deep breath before I started my slide presentation. This was going to be the longest hour of my life.

"Well, you'll be pleased to know that Cambridge Athletics hired us to do their campaign," I said as I waddled into the kitchen that night, red-faced and throbbing with arousal. David turned his attention from the pots and pans to me, grinning.

"I knew you could do it! Celebratory curry sound good?"

"I don't want a fucking curry, David. I want your cock inside me, because I feel like I might explode if you don't make love to me right here, right now."

Despite briefly looking like he'd protest, David's eyes glazed over with the sudden onset of lust. He dropped his spoon on the kitchen counter and strode toward me, pushing me up against the red brick wall in our kitchen. His beard prickled as his lips met mine.

We kissed hungrily, messily, hands roving over bodies as if we were lovers who hadn't seen each other in months. You could say we hadn't—not like this. I pulled his shirt from his trousers and unbuttoned it with such ferocity, buttons came loose and clanked onto the floor.

I felt gone, lost to a surge of delirium as David hiked my skirt up and pulled down my panties. I stepped out of them gratefully, glad to be freed and glad to feel his big fingers slipping between my plump lips.

He made an admiring noise as two fingers circled around my clit, eliciting moans from me that made my knees buckle.

"Such a lovely side effect of two inconspicuous love balls."

I felt tongue-tied, like I'd temporarily forgotten how to speak English. My body reverted to its basest functions, my pussy grinding itself against David's nimble fingers and hand. When he withdrew them, I watched through the glaze of pent-up lust as he licked my juices off his fingertips. He was practically drenched with me.

Then he grinned. I didn't need anything more than his grin and the sight of that tongue. I unbuckled his belt and nearly attacked his trousers, revealing first boxers then—oh, hallelujah—the sight of his erect cock, proudly jutting out from the thatch of curly hairs just below his belly.

He pushed my legs apart with his knees, turning me around and wriggling to get me into the right position. He took his cock in his hands and guided it into me, my wet labia instantly coating it with my juices. A muffled gasp was followed by the relief of feeling him fill me so perfectly, unlike the love balls that had been taunting me all day. Speaking of those...

"You took the love balls out, didn't you?" he whispered into my ear.

I chuckled. "I guess I wanted something a bit *meatier* inside me."

"Cheeky mare."

In a flash, one of his big hands smacked down on my ass. An electric, red-hot current sizzled through me, almost making me tip over the edge into my climax. My pussy clenched around him, making us both moan in turn. I gave over to him, laughing elatedly as his cock slid out and slammed back into me.

One hand tangled in my wild red hair, pulling gently but firmly enough to make me shiver. The other snaked around to play with my swollen clit. My knuckles were nearly white from having to brace myself against the brickwork.

David's softness pressing against my back was a contrast to the sharp, hard movements his hips were making. His cock had me open wide, the tip of him brushing past my sensitive G-spot with every thrust.

He let go of my hair and shifted his arm down to my breasts, relishing the feel of my pert nipples. It was crystal clear that I wasn't going to last a very long time, but every muscle in my body seemed hell-bent on making this sensation last forever. This wasn't easy to do, especially with the feeling of David being everywhere at once: playing with my nipples, driving his cock into me, frigging me toward the orgasm I'd been craving from him.

And then he whispered in my ear, "I dare you to let go, Kat. Let go of everything. Come for me, baby. Come for me. Come."

The pressure on my clit and the pressure inside me, combined with his soft voice repeating that delirious mantra, made everything burst. My pussy, along with my body, clenched into an almighty roar, which echoed even in our spacious kitchen. I didn't know how long it lasted; could have been seconds, could have been days.

David continued his thrusts, manically in search of his own release. His sharp, sure movements became an erratic frenzy until I could feel his fingers digging into my hips, almost pulling me onto his pulsing cock as he emptied himself into me with a caveman roar.

He slumped, taking me into his big arms as his cock twitched itself out still inside me. And my clit was still crying out for more. But the rest of my body felt spent.

"David." I slurred. "Food. Water."

He let out a long moan and hugged me tight. "No. I don't want to let you go."

"The curry, David."

"I still don't want to let you go. It's been too long since...and all these dares, just making me want to ravish you more. I love you so much. Can't believe I get to marry you."

As if I didn't feel like I'd melted enough. "Two weeks. We mustn't let stress get in the way of us again. I'm too fond of your naked body and your magnificent cock for that."

As we rearranged ourselves and sat down for dinner, cuddled up on the couch in front of the television, David's face suddenly lit up, making him look like Hannibal from *The A-Team* whenever he had a plan.

"I've just come up with the perfect dare."

The dinner was going just about as well as planned, in that Greg hadn't offended anyone yet and the food was absolutely beautiful. To my surprise, I wasn't feeling stressed at all. But that was mainly because David and I had been shagging like rabbits for the past two weeks. We hadn't taken our hands off each other.

My new husband's hands, by coincidence, were snaking around my waist in a hug. "Are you holding up okay?" he said, kissing my neck and swaying me in time to the music.

"Yeah, I'm good. I did meet a scary lady earlier on. Your side of the family, I think? Talks about blood a lot?"

"Ah. You've met Aunty Bette then."

"I wish I hadn't."

We watched the crowd for a few moments; friends and family uniting, dancing awkwardly and having fun. David and I exchanged a secret smile.

"Are you ready to give your speech, my love?"

"That depends. Are you ready to take the controls?"

David slyly revealed a little remote, stashed away in his pocket. "Ready when you are."

"You better fucking ravish me later on. I'm going to need it."

"It's our wedding night. I'm planning on a hell of a lot more than just ravishing you. You best be ready..."

"Is that a dare?"

"No. It's a guarantee."

He winked, causing a happy flutter in my stomach. I was looking forward to married life already. If we could spend the rest of our lives naked and in bed, I wouldn't object.

But before that, I needed to make a speech. I strode to the stage, not yet anticipating David flipping the switch.

"Thank you for coming, everyone. It means A LOT!"

At the back of the room, David just winked at me.

THE PROTOTYPE

Malin James

W hat the hell is that?"

"It's a prototype," Edward says, grinning like a kid.

"For what?"

I ask because the form and function of the thing in Edward's hand remains unclear. For all intents and purposes, it looks like a beach ball that's been shoved through a piece of three-quarter-inch plastic pipe. The pipe forms a sort of handle—I can tell because that's where he's holding it—while the uninflated ball flops out the other side, all strangled and primary colored. He has a bright-red bicycle pump clutched in his other hand.

"It's something I'm making. For you."

Edward smiles at me. His eyes, behind his glasses, are earnest and adorable. Edward invents things for fun. In real life, he does something abstract with currency markets, but in his dreams he has an underground lab and a henchman. At the moment, he's wearing his *eureka!* face, which means he's onto something.

"That's really sweet, babe," I say, coming closer. "But I'm not sure what I'm going to do with a ball shoved through a tube."

"Ah," he replies, "but it's not *just* a ball shoved through a tube. Watch!"

Edward holds out the contraption, which is, apparently, more than it seems, and rummages around in the "handle" before pulling out the ball's valve. Then he attaches the bicycle pump. Cradling it like a baby, he lays the prototype on the counter and pumps the ball full of air. Once the ball is inflated, it sticks awkwardly out from the top of the plastic rod like a...like an I don't know the hell what. Then he looks at me, triumphant. He's so jazzed he's nearly rocking on his heels. With a grin, he presents it to me like a bouquet.

"See?"

"Uh...yeah, babe. I see."

I reach out and accept it, holding it awkwardly, like an unsuspecting bridesmaid after the toss.

"But what do I do with it?"

Edward gives me the look he always gives me when he can't believe I'm serious. Last time I got it, I'd confessed to not liking Queen.

"Really, Jess. Think."

I give him what amounts to a very blank stare.

"C'mon, babe," he says, adjusting his glasses. (Edward's really cute when he's exasperated). "Use your imagination."

He stares at me meaningfully. I stare back. Then I notice the lusty glint in his eyes. Okay, I think, meeting his lusty glint with my own. That's a quality hint. Clearly, its use isn't purely academic. I study the prototype.

The plastic handle is smooth, with rounded edges, and the ball is one of the pricier kinds that doesn't have any seams. Still, it's just a rod with a ball shoved through it—a ball that, when filled, bulges obscenely out from one end. I still don't know what it's *supposed* to do, but it sure could fill a girl...I gasp. Suddenly, it clicks.

"Oh my god. *Really?*"

I stare at my boyfriend. He grins.

"Yeah. Wanna try it out?"

The look on his face is all I need. My belly flutters, and I go syrupy inside.

"Yeah. I really do."

"Good," he says, taking the prototype back. "Then come to the bedroom with me."

Edward takes my hand and leads me down the hall. He's looking at me with his sweet, hungry eyes and rubbing my palm with his thumb. When we finally reach the bedroom, he puts the prototype down and kisses me full on the mouth.

"Sure you want to do this?"

"Oh, you know me and science..." It's a little hard to breathe with him nuzzling my skin.

"Yeah," he says, nipping my ear. "Now, take off your clothes."

I slip out of my shirt and bra, like a good little guinea pig. The room's chilly, but when my nipples peak, it's from arousal, not the cold. I unbuckle my belt and slide down my jeans, but when I go to slip off my panties, Edward pulls me close.

"Here, let me."

Without taking his eyes off me, Edward slips his fingers into the waistband of my panties and slowly draws them down. Then he plants a kiss on my hip bone before tossing them aside.

"Okay, Jess. Lie down. I want to see how wet you are."

He's excited, but judging by his tone, which is more clinical than sexy-sexy, it's the prototype that's got him hot. Suddenly nervous, I lie down and watch him kick off his shoes (Edward never wears shoes on the bed). Then he gently parts my legs. They fall open, inviting, as he fingers my damp curls. I shiver again.

"Cold?" he whispers.

I shake my head.

"Nervous?"

"A little bit."

He nods, slicking his fingertips over my folds. I'm wetter than I should be, under the circumstances.

"Don't worry, Jess. I'll take care of you. I know how you love to be filled."

Still fully dressed, he kneels between my legs and slowly licks up one side of my slit before licking down the other. I gasp and move my hips, but he holds me steady. Then he goes to work with his tongue.

Let's be clear. In addition to being good at doing abstract things with currencies, Edward has a brilliantly filthy mind, as evidenced by the gadget he's about to use on me. He is also, I should say, incredibly good at licking my clit. Tiny circles, slow sucks, little whorls just beneath the hood. The man is a multi-talented genius and I, lucky girl that I am, am in the middle of benefiting from not one, but two of my genius's talents.

He's at me for less than two minutes when my breath catches and I start to moan. That's when he raises his head.

"How're you doing, Jess? Feeling good?"

He gives me a cheeky grin before pressing his lips to my cunt. I shudder and mewl a protest when he lifts himself away.

"Hold that thought."

Before I can do more than whimper, Edward grabs the proto-type and a bottle of lube. Working with scientific precision, he slicks the ball's cheerful, tricolored surface, which is flaccid and crinkly and not sexy at all. In fact, nothing about it is sexy. It's just kind of weird. I shift, trying to recapture the hum between my legs, but I'm starting to feel weird too. My boyfriend is going to stick a beach ball up my cooch. That's just fucking weird.

Determined not to blow the experiment, I focus on Edward instead, slicking away with a crease in his brow. *He's adorable,* I think. The hum picks back up again. Finally, when the ball is dripping wet, he lays the prototype down on a towel.

Working quickly, as if I'm a soufflé he's afraid will fall, Edward pulls back on a little string at the top of the plastic tube, loading the handle with the ball...sort of like a tampon. Definitely weird. Then he attaches the bicycle pump to the valve of the ball, which is peeking out the bottom.

"Okay, Jess," he says, holding up the loaded tube. He looks like he should be wearing goggles and rubber gloves. "I'm going to insert this into you," he says, jiggling the device. "It might be a little strange but it shouldn't hurt. Just relax."

Yeah. Sure. I nod.

Suddenly, Edward isn't my boyfriend. He's Einstein, or Tesla, or Edison...if any of those guys had bothered with sex toys. I breathe in slowly and exhale, trying to remember what my sister said about Lamaze, which is dumb because she had something coming out, and I've got something going in.

Edward is gentle but firm as he guides the plastic tube in past my pussy lips. As nervous as I am, it slides into me easily, meeting with little resistance. (Edward the Inventor turns me on almost as much as Edward the Boyfriend). Then he twists the tube.

"Okay, Jess. I'm going to deploy the ball now."

"Oh yeah, baby."

He grins sheepishly.

"Sorry, babe. Almost there."

At this point, the haze of arousal that Edward's tongue inspired has been destroyed by the strangeness of what's happening between my legs. I give him a look. He pats my leg.

"I promise. Almost there."

Suddenly, I feel the tube leave my body as Edward pulls it back, leaving the ball in place. Now that the ball is "deployed," the tube is a handle again. This definitely feels weird. Not terrible, but not good. By now, I'm impatient, which Edward can probably sense. I'm about to tell him the prototype's a dud when he takes the bicycle pump and begins to inflate the ball.

I gasp. With each pump of air, the ball gets bigger—first the size of two fingers, then four, then the size of a small cock, then a large cock, then a large dildo, and then a fist, and all the while it's conforming to my shape as it fills me. By the time Edward stops pumping, the ball has become the best, most tailored, most *perfect* fill—most perfect fuck, even—I have ever had.

I'm panting as I stare at him with eyes that must be totally glazed. It feels so good that I'm afraid to move. It's just sitting there inside me—pressing against my G-spot and all four walls at once—and I'm almost halfway there. The last thing I want to do is dislodge it. Edward watches me with his scientist look, taking in the sweat that's beading my brow and my short, rapid breaths.

"How's that feel, Jess? Good?"

I nod. He raises a brow. He's enjoying the fact that I can't answer.

"Okay. Tell me how *this* feels…"

Gently, Edward takes the prototype's handle and turns it, very slightly. I moan as that bare hint of movement shoots straight through to my limbs.

"Good. Now, how about this?"

Slowly, slowly, Edward pulls the prototype out as my hips rise in protest. Then, just as slowly, he plunges it back in. Some sort of guttural sound drags itself out of my lungs as my back arches against this weird, perfect, glorious device. He pulls it out again, a bit farther this time, before thrusting it back in. Back and forth, back and forth. Each time, he takes it farther, makes it sweeter, as the contraption fills me like nothing I've ever felt. All around it, my muscles pulse and clutch. I'm breathing so hard that I'm afraid I might pass out.

Sensing how close I am, Edward keeps working the prototype with one hand while he touches my clit with the other. I buck up, accidentally pushing the prototype up on my G-spot as I rub against the pad of his thumb, which is circling my clit. I can't hear anymore—there's too much blood rushing in my ears, too much breathing, too many impulses firing away beneath my skin, too much, too much, too much. Edward keeps up the pressure on my clit as he thrusts the prototype into me. One more long, slow pull, and I come.

It's one of the best fucking orgasms of my life. Filthy and aching, it spills through me, filling my arms and legs and lungs. My hips thrust against Edward's invention desperately, of their own accord, clutching at the sweet, giving pressure of the ridiculous little thing.

Edward stills his hand as I come back down. Every cell in my body feels like it's been fucked. I have never been so exhausted, or so satisfied. Edward opens the valve and lets the air out of the ball. Then he gently strokes my hair and kisses my face while, inside of me, the prototype shrinks and deflates until he's able to easily pull it out.

"So, Jess," he says, studying me like I'm the prettiest petri dish in the world. "What do you think?"

I'm still panting as I stroke his sweet, flushed face. Despite his obvious hard-on, he looks as drowsy and spent as I feel.

"Babe, I think you're a genius. Get a patent on that thing."

ICY BED

J. Crichton

The lights are dim and the television is playing on mute in the background just to keep the sense of aloneness at bay. You turn on your laptop and wait for the telltale ringing of a video call so that you can see your beloved's face once more. He's been away on business for so long already—too long. Though you were happy for him when he first got the promotion, you've started to wonder if it was such a good idea after all. He smiles and strokes the corners of the screen as though he could touch you through it and then asks you about your day, in spite of the lines of exhaustion etched on his face.

"They've got me stuck here for another week, sweetheart," he says from the tiny screen you're watching him through. It's more like an apology than anything else, but it's already been two weeks and you don't know how long you can keep going.

"I miss sleeping next to you," you say, fixing the straps on your tank top and looking sufficiently pouty at the web camera to make him feel guilty. It's not his fault, but you're sitting there in your pajamas and he's a plane ride away in a business suit. Someone's gotta pay, right?

"I know," he says regretfully, kicking off his shoes so he can drag the laptop onto the bed, just like you. "Every night I'm here I go to sleep thinking of touching you. I want to kiss that pretty mouth of yours again and make love to you. Do you miss that too?"

"Of course I do," you say as your clit gives a hopeful throb. You're up and in the closet again, picking out the shirt he wore the last time you saw him in person. It looks exactly like the white tailored number he's wearing right now, but it smells like him and you want it close. Right in front of the camera you pull off your tank top, exposing your breasts as you slide the button-up over your shoulders and leave it open.

There's a sharp inhalation as his eyes watch you, mesmerized. "Take them off," he demands, voice shaky. "The pants—take them off. I only want you to be wearing my shirt. Please."

You comply, getting up onto your knees and pulling them down so he can briefly glimpse your freshly waxed mound. The laptop is off his lap now and the man who should be on top of you is stroking himself through his trousers.

"Open them," you say. "Undo the zipper and take your cock out, but don't you dare take those pants off. If you come all over yourself you'll just have to explain it to the dry cleaners tomorrow."

His eyes widen and he chuckles breathlessly. "As you wish." The long smooth shaft appears and you're nearly salivating. It's been so long since you tasted that gorgeous head or licked at the vein that runs along the underside. His forefinger and thumb are rolling the skin idly just as your own digits move south, playing and teasing but not much more—yet.

Your right hand is on your breast, tugging at your nipples

while you lift the edges of your shirt, showing him your pussy again.

"Such a shame that you can't touch, isn't it?" you tease him. "Where's your ice bucket?"

"By the minibar." He's jerking off a little more earnestly now. "I'll go get it if you do…"

So there's a pause as you go to the fridge and pick out a few ice cubes, stopping by the bedroom closet again for your bag of toys. Usually you use them together, but needs must.

You hold an ice cube between your breasts and brush it across the stiff peaks of your nipples, shivering as the ice melts enough to qualify you for a wet T-shirt contest. The half-done cube travels down your tummy and between your legs, where you hold it just close enough to make you jump.

He's moaning now, telling you how hot you are and how he can't wait to be inside you. You tell him to stroke himself with an ice cube too, and watch little trickles of cold water run down his dick and pool in his pubic hair.

"Spread your legs for me, baby," he pleads. There are beads of sweat beginning to form on his forehead. His tie is hanging loose around his neck and his left hand has also strayed to his nipples, where you love to lick and bite. "I want to see that beautiful hole."

And then your legs are in a V-shape on either side of the screen and you're holding yourself open wide, imagining his tongue inside you, or his fingers. You balance the remnants of an ice cube right at your hole and then push it inside, fighting to keep your thighs from clenching together at the cold. Water's trickling down onto the bed just as a fat drop of precome appears on the bright-red head of his dick.

"I want to fuck you so bad, sweetheart," he says hoarsely. There's emotion in his voice, and not just from the effort of holding back. "You're glistening, I can see it from here."

You smile and stick a finger inside yourself, showing him just how wet you are before you reach back into the bag and grab a tiny vibrator that slips like a cuff over the end of your finger. "Soon," you say, "but not soon enough."

Your hips jump against the sensation, spread as they are, but you're not soft on yourself. You may squirm against the pleasure, but you're going to take it and he's going to watch. His hand has slowed and he's tucked his shirt; watching you stroke your own clit has him open mouthed and panting.

"Don't come yet," he says, just as you feel your sex squeeze. It's an effort to draw yourself back, but you're listening, especially when that great big cock is twitching right in front of the camera.

"Can you get that pink dong out of the toy bag?" he asks. You do, and you're just about to ask what he wants you to do with it when his phone rings. A look of panic comes over his face as he tells you it's work, then proceeds to answer it with his junk hanging out and his wedding ring still glinting on his finger.

You set the dong—one with balls, so that it can sit upright—in the space in front of the keyboard. You get on your hands and knees and you deep-throat it, even though it's plastic and it doesn't taste a thing like him. You want to anyway, because he's discussing a business deal but he's also watching, and the force of his reaction is strong enough that he has to squeeze the base of his cock to keep from spurting.

Your finger vibrator goes back between your legs as you swallow this surrogate dick and soon you're coming, moaning around the rim and sinking into the sheets.

"Yes, okay. See you to-tomorrow, sir," he manages gruffly. The tie has gone missing somewhere, and he drifts out of view again. You can hear the sound of his suitcase being unzipped, rummaging—but what is he doing?

"Hurry up," you say, just as he comes back with a pair of your best panties in his hand and a little travel-sized bottle of lube in the other.

"When did you steal those?"

"I got them out of your drawer right before I left." He wraps the silky pink undergarment around himself and covers it liberally in lube. Watching him slide in and out of the fabric has you jealous so you set the dong upright again, holding it steady with your feet as you lower yourself down onto it.

"You're doing the laundry when you get back," you groan, happy to be finally filled like you haven't been the past couple of weeks. "Oh god, I wish it was you fucking me right now. It's so big, baby, it's such a tight fit."

"I'm gonna," he promises, fisting his cock hard and fast. "When I get home you're not going to walk for days—and we won't leave the bedroom for days, either."

Your fingers are back to your clit now, stroking the pink nub as your body pulls the dong in farther. You squeeze and knead your breasts for the camera, just for him to see, and you watch him jerking his cock—your cock, it belongs to you. You can smell him on his shirt and hear his voice and you're coming so hard as you bounce up and down on the toy you two usually play with together that you're seeing stars.

When your vision clears there's a white ribbonlike mess over the picture that your husband is hastily wiping at with a tissue.

With a laugh, you ask, "Why did you bring a pair of my underwear with you, anyway?"

"A lot of the guys I travel with are up for getting a piece on the side wherever we go. I just choose to take my piece with me."

"That's very sweet," you say with a smile, lifting yourself off of a dick that isn't going to soften inside you anytime soon. "I think we've found our nightly solution for when you're away, my love."

SURPRISE

Katya Harris

I have a surprise for you."

In the middle of fixing his tie, Gage looked over at Hanna. Interest sparkled in his winter-blue eyes. "I thought we weren't doing gifts this year."

Tonight was their second anniversary and they had both agreed that, what with the cost of moving into their new home, presents could wait until next year. Instead, they were taking a break from the redecorating that had taken over their lives, and going out to dinner to celebrate.

"I couldn't resist," Hanna told him. She shrugged. "It's only something small." A sly smile pulled at the corner of her mouth. "And it's for the both of us."

Smoothing down his tie, Gage turned to her. Hanna's mouth went dry, the spark of lust that had been lighting her up all day intensifying to a flickering flame in her belly. Damn, he was fine, what her grandmother would call a tall drink of cool water.

"Do I get to see what it is?" he asked, walking over to her.

Resting a hand on his chest, her thumb drawing a caress just above his heart, she went up on tiptoe and brushed a kiss over his firm lips. "What are you going to do to convince me?" she teased.

Large hands circled her waist, pulling her closer. The heat of his body enveloped over her, and Hanna breathed in the delicious smell of his freshly showered skin mixed with the citrus tang of his aftershave.

Gage rubbed his lips along her shoulder to her neck, drifting soft kisses along the sensitive curve bared by her strapless dress. "I'm sure I could think of a way."

Hanna's knees went weak. Her hands moved up, one gripping her husband's shoulder, the one holding the box resting on the other. Slanting her head to give him better access, she sighed as pleasure gilded her veins. "You're spoiling my plans."

Trailing more kisses up Hanna's throat and along her jaw, Gage licked at her lips. She opened for him and his tongue slipped inside. He kissed her delicately, careful of her red lipstick. "Would you really mind?"

Probably not, Hanna thought, but a little resistance now would mean greater rewards later.

Slipping free of Gage's embrace, Hanna walked over to their bed. Putting down the box, she turned to him and asked, "Don't you want to open it?"

Arousal was a banked heat in Gage's eyes. He stalked over to her, his suit trousers doing nothing to hide the erection that rode down his left pant leg. She'd have to remind him to bring his jacket tonight.

The box wasn't big, about the size of a shoebox, and was wrapped in pearlescent white paper with a large gold silk bow. Hanna watched with mounting excitement as Gage tore open the wrapping paper. When he pulled the top off the box, revealing its contents, her pussy fluttered in time with her quickened pulse.

From the side, she slipped her arms around his waist. Leaning her head against his chest, Hanna's eyes were fixed on the box's contents and Gage's hands as they hovered over it, unsure.

"Do you like it?"

Tension was a fine hum beneath Gage's skin. "Um, what am I looking at, Hanna?"

Smoothing her hand down Gage's stomach, she palmed his cock. He was still hard, the engorged length of him firm against her hand despite his apparent unease. Gage moaned, a soft rumble, his hips moving to push his erection harder against her stroking hand.

"You know what it is," Hanna told him softly. They'd laughingly teased each other about getting one a couple of times, both of them blushing and fairly squirming with excitement before they tumbled into bed for a bout of hectic lovemaking. Hanna had decided it was time to stop talking about it.

Deft flicks of her fingers undid his belt and unfastened his trousers. Plunging her hand into his boxers, she cupped the heavy globes of his balls. As always, a little thrill went through her as she rolled the smooth sac in her palm. God, she loved that he shaved down there. His skin was so soft and delicate beneath her fingertips, so vulnerable where the rest of him was so hard.

Gage's body tightened; he began to quietly pant. He shifted his stance, widening his legs, and with a grin Hanna slid her hand lower, the pads of her fingers rubbing over the silky skin of his perineum. His hips bobbed back and forth in his mounting excitement, and Hanna's fingertips brushed the rim of his asshole. A sharp groan shuddered past Gage's lips.

"You like it, don't you darling?" she asked huskily. "When I play with you here?" Her slender hand burrowed farther between his legs, her fingers circling the tight pucker of his asshole. It flexed beneath her touch, an intimate kiss.

"So this is for me then?" Gage asked shakily.

Hanna nodded. She couldn't look away from where her wrist disappeared between her husband's legs. Her panties were soaked through, her pussy aching for his ruddy cock, which was straining upward, moisture glistening on the swollen crown. "Yes. Just think," she said in her best temptress voice. "Going out tonight, your ass crammed full with that plug. Sitting and eating dinner in a room full of other people while it's inside you." Her finger pushed lightly against the dimple of his asshole, and she bit her bottom lip in breathless pleasure when he bore down and let her in. The tip of her finger slipped easily into his rear even without lubrication.

Gage groaned, a heavy animalistic sound. His sock-covered feet flexed, his body rocking on the small intrusion of her finger. Precome leaked from the tip of his cock, dribbling down its sides like melting ice cream from a cone. Hanna's mouth watered to lick it up.

"You're torturing me," Gage moaned.

Slowing pumping her finger in and out of him, Hanna looked up at Gage's face. The muscles in his jaw were clenched tight and sweat dampened the dark hair at his temples. "Shall I do it some more?"

His answer was rasped out on a harsh breath. "Oh god, yes."

Hanna grinned.

Without moving her hand or breaking the decadent rhythm of her finger, Hanna swung round and dropped to her knees. She licked up the sides of Gage's cock, chasing the dribbles of his salty-sweet precome. The musky taste of him filled her senses, and she pushed in hard with her finger, wriggling it in his depths.

Gage groaned. His hands flew up to tangle in her hair and Hanna back away slightly. "No touching," she told him. "I don't want you to ruin my hair."

She couldn't give a damn about her neat up-do though. It was the frustrated look in Gage's eyes she cared about, the tension that bracketed his tightly pursed mouth. His hands fisted, returned slowly to his sides. Keeping her gaze locked with his, Hanna leaned forward and licked across the tip of his dick with a slow swipe of her tongue. Gage's eyes narrowed, frustration pinching the smooth skin between his eyebrows.

"Will you let me?" she asked.

Gage knew what she was talking about. "Persuade me some more."

Hanna sucked the ripe plum of his cockhead into her mouth. He made a noise somewhere between a growl and a squeal, a sound so undignified Hanna didn't need to look up to know he was blushing.

Her finger kept in time as she bobbed her head up and down on the end of Gage's cock. Her tongue flickered over and caressed the silky skin of his shaft, the tip tickling at the spot beneath the crown that always made him shudder in pleasure.

When Gage began to thrust forward, she released his dick with a final lavish lick.

Looking up with a coy tilt of her head, she asked, "So?"

He looked half-mad, his eyes wild and his features taut with the intensity of his lust. Exactly how Hanna wanted him. Her body throbbed with excitement.

"You really want this?" Gage's voice was a harsh rasp.

A quick lick to the weeping slit of his cock; one more pump of her finger before she slipped it free. "Yes." She smiled up at him. "You do too." He sucked in a breath, but didn't deny it.

Rolling up on to her feet, Hanna kissed him. "Bend over,"

she whispered against his lips. "Put your hands on the bed."

She stepped out of the way and watched as, after a beat of hesitation, Gage did it. He spread his legs as wide as he could with his trousers falling down around his ankles. Hanna was just about to ask him to raise his ass up, when he lifted it up all on his own.

"I knew you'd want this."

Looking over his shoulder, Gage speared her with a heated look that was an equal mix of arousal and frustration. "Then you know what I'm going to be doing to you later."

Delight shivered over Hanna's skin. "Darling," she purred. "I'm looking forward to it."

Picking up the plug, Hanna caressed the black silicone. She delighted in the smooth feel of it, the dense weight that would soon fill Gage's ass. Hanna had bought it a week ago and it had been torture thinking of it sitting in its box.

A small bottle of lube had been nestled in the box too, and Hanna used it, squeezing some onto the tip of the plug. With her finger, she smeared it around the plug's surface.

"Hold yourself open for me, baby."

Gage's breathing was loud in the quiet, his smothered groan harsh. He rested his forehead on the bed, his hands reaching back to pull the cheeks of his ass wide apart. Bending forward at the waist, Hanna licked at the dainty rosebud of his asshole.

"Holy fuck!" Gage shouted at the first touch of her tongue. His body jerked like she'd electrocuted him, a full-body convulsion that ended with him pressing back into her lewd, open-mouthed kiss. "Jesus Christ, Hanna, what are you trying to do to me?"

Her answer was a smile against his skin as she gently laved him with the flat of her tongue. Over and over, she licked at his asshole, wetting it completely. "I'm getting you ready. I thought you might like this better than just the lube."

"If you keep doing that," Gage said shakily, "I'm going to come."

Hanna backed off enough to say, "I'm almost done. I just want to do this." Dipping her head, she jabbed into his ass with her stiffened tongue, wriggling it around in the hot, tight tunnel.

Gage yelled out and he did it again when she drew back, quickly notched the tip of the plug at his entrance and started to push it into him. He shook, his fingers digging into his own flesh. Expletives fell from his lips, carried on gusting groans. Hanna worked the plug into him with slow thrusts, going a little deeper each time. She could have moved more quickly, Gage certainly wanted to; his shattered voice begged for more. When that didn't work, he growled, "Shove that fucking thing in me now, Hanna!"

With a grin, Hanna did what he wanted. A hard shove and the body of the plug disappeared into his ass, his anus closing greedily around the tapered stem, the base running smoothly along Gage's crack except for the small silver bump at its center.

A choked sound was squeezed out of Gage's rigid body. Hanna wanted to stroke him, but her hands were slick with lube. Blanketing his body with hers, she made soothing nonsensical noises to help him calm down. The tension slowly ebbed from his muscles, although it didn't fade completely. His hands shook slightly as he straightened his clothes, his fingers fumbling with the fastenings as he covered his rigidly hard erection. He didn't seem to realize that his dick was still smeared with red from her lipstick.

"How does it feel?"

Gage's eyes were wide, stark white surrounding the blazing

blue. Sweat dotted his upper lip. At his sides, his fists clenched and unclenched. "Good," he finally breathed. He moved gingerly, and a shudder racked his frame. His eyes fluttered shut. "Full."

Hanna brushed the back of her hand over his steel-hard cock pressing against the front of his slacks. With a strangled sound, Gage jerked away. "Don't. I'll come."

Perfect.

Rolling up onto her tiptoes, Hanna brushed a kiss across his mouth. "Let me fix my makeup, and then we can go."

His nod was abrupt.

Going into the bathroom, Hanna cleaned the lube from her hands, reapplied her makeup and smoothed her lightly mussed hair. It took her barely five minutes. Excitement fizzed in her blood, her clit humming with arousal so badly it burned with a bright delicious pain. Her panties clung to the folds of her pussy, soaked through with her juices. She wriggled out of them, depositing the useless scrap of silk in the laundry, before she walked out of the bathroom.

Gage was waiting for her. He'd tidied himself up, slipped on his suit jacket and overcoat. Anyone looking at him would think he was calm and collected, but Hanna could see the tension bracketing his mouth, the wild glimmer that darted in and out of his eyes.

"Are you ready?"

Hanna smiled at his gruff question, lifting an eyebrow teasingly. "Are you?"

An answering smile flickered at the corner of Gage's mouth. "You're loving this."

Walking past him, Hanna blew him a kiss. "Only as much as you are."

Catching her with an arm around her waist, Gage pulled her to him and brushed his lips lightly over hers.

"Mind my lipstick," Hanna told him breathlessly.

Gage wiped a hand over his lips, erasing the traces of red that clung there. "Come on, let's have dinner."

Hand in hand they walked to the front door. Gage helped her into her coat. He turned to open the door and that was when Hanna reached into her pocket.

Gage fell against the door frame, gasping in deep gulping breaths. His body convulsed and then slumped forward when Hanna took her finger off the button she had secreted in her coat earlier.

Red streaked Gage's cheekbones. "What the fuck was that?"

Hanna painted an innocent expression on her face. "Oh, did I forget to tell you? The plug vibrates." Walking past him and out of the door, she took the remote out of her pocket and showed it to him. She grinned, wide and wicked. "We're going to have quite the night, baby."

THE SUPERMAN
DILDO

E. Bellamy

I was a math major, but only because I was good at geometry. At the University of New England, a small Maine school walking distance from the ocean, I spent hours upon hours hunched over graph paper, punching numbers into calculators and warding off the mathematical mind that haunted me, reminding me in specific numbers just how much of my life I was wasting on theorems and cosine. I did the math: I was getting laid zero percent of the time.

This meant many things, but mostly it meant a lot of masturbating. My roommate Gerard would go to class and I'd tear off my Levi's and touch myself, thinking of women stretched on my bed, their pink vaginas wet with desire, their stomachs and tits moistened with my saliva. I'd stroke until I came into a sock or balled up corner of bedsheet. Although there's no math to prove it, there's only so much jerking off you can do before you go insane.

* * *

One Friday night, I was out for a beer at a bar in the old mill buildings with Gerard to see a riot girl punk band called Toilet. Gerard, a drinking buddy and fellow math major, knew how horny I was, so he decided to take me out. Even just *talking* with him about getting laid made my cock nestle, erect and firm, inside my left pant leg.

We each grabbed a pint of an amber ale and stood talking by the bar, waiting for the band to take the stage. Gerard was scoping out attractive women and men. He checked out men to size himself up against the competition.

Then a bass thumped and the crowd's attention turned to the small stage. The singer, in a small red dress that hugged her hips and tits, danced onto the stage. Her range was astounding, and her tone was high and raspy, like a young, punk Janis Joplin. She had long, black hair with blonde streaks like rays of sun. She was voluptuous and curvy. I studied the perfect geometric shapes of her: the sidelong ovals of her ass and breasts and the ridges of her thick lips as she danced around the stage with the energy of someone dancing to her favorite album in the privacy of her bedroom.

I was staring. I had to meet her.

"You like her?" Gerard asked, nudging me.

"Yes."

"Well, stick around," he said. "She'll have a drink after the set."

"How do you know that?" I asked.

"Because, dude. That's Kelly Juarez. She's in my philosophy class."

I took a long sip of beer and placed the empty pint glass on the bar.

"And get this, dude," Gerard said, grabbing my arm. "She said she wants to meet you."

If I'd still been drinking, I would have spit out my drink in disbelief.

I ordered another beer. I wanted to meet Kelly, and perhaps even ask her out for coffee. I also wanted to stay and pick Gerard's brain. I asked him why she would want to meet me, and he said something about her knowing I was a math tutor, and that she found me cute.

"How could she like me?" I asked. "I have this protruding gut, and my wardrobe consists mostly of shirts with superhero logos on them."

"I don't know, man," he said. "Word on the street is she's really into geeks."

Kelly and I hit it off from the first beer. We drank one and left Gerard at the bar with his dozens of prospects so we could walk alone by the beach. Kelly said she loved the beach for its serenity, for the thoughts it evoked. She wrote all of her music by the beach, just staring at the waves.

But it was too chilly to be by the ocean that night. I suggested we go back to my room for chamomile tea and blankets. We sat on the floor, swaddled ourselves in knit shawls and held our hands against our porcelain mugs, talking about our individual passions. She talked about the evolution of girls in punk rock, from Patti Smith to Potty Mouth. I commented on string theory and cryptology, and as the discussion reached the pinnacle of its complexity, she threw her hands on me.

"Fuck me," she said, squeezing my thigh. I wasn't expecting such a quick move, but I was certainly into it.

She pulled her shirt up so I could see her breasts. My cock immediately stiffened. I yanked her panties to her ankles. I ran my hands up her smooth leg to her pussy, rubbing the wet skin of her labia.

"Wait," she said, pushing herself up. "I want you to use something."

She reached into her purse and pulled out a dildo. She handed it to me, and I examined it closely. It wasn't just a dildo—it was a dildo with a Superman illustration on it. A Superman dildo. It was painted to look just like him, with a cape and everything. My eyes shifted back and forth between Kelly and the Superman dildo.

"It gets me off every time," she said. "I just love Superman."

Kelly looked so beautiful bathed in the low lighting of my desk lamp. I wanted to continue stripping and touching each other, but for some reason the dildo put me in a strange mood. I didn't want Clark Kent to be partially responsible for getting Kelly off. I wanted to slide warmly inside of her and make her come all by myself. I wanted to be her superhero.

"Maybe we should take things slow," I said, handing her the dildo.

"Okay," she said, nodding. "Okay, yeah. That might be good." She kept her eyes focused on her hands, twisting them in contemplation. Her cheeks blushed in humiliation. She stood. "I guess I should go. I'm tired and should get some sleep." I didn't want her to go, but couldn't really argue with her sudden mood swing. I felt guilt in the pit of my stomach. I could tell she felt embarrassed.

I walked her to my door. Just before she could exit, I leaned into her and kissed her on the cheek, smelling the floral scent of her shampoo. I wanted more, but I didn't say anything. I watched her walk down the corridor.

"Good night," I said.

She turned and waved with the dildo.

* * *

As the weeks moseyed on, we alternated between dates and tutoring sessions. By day, I would help her with her math and chemistry homework. By night, we indulged in our nerdy hobbies like playing video games, reading comic books and watching sci-fi television shows. But to my discontent, we never had sex. We didn't even try. Not since the Superman dildo night.

I hated the sound of that: *Superman dildo night.*

I tried really hard to get Kelly in the mood. I would play Marvin Gaye and Lou Reed and light candles and nibble on her neck, but nothing seemed to make her feel sexy. I figured she was embarrassed.

Then one night, Kelly turned off our *Doctor Who* episode right in the middle. I looked at her, curious.

"I need to know. Did the dildo freak you out?" she asked, running a finger along my forearm. "You can be honest with me."

"A little," I admitted. "Maybe 'freaked' is the wrong word."

"Well, why didn't you tell me?"

I told her that it was complicated. I told her I didn't want to use a dildo on her because I wanted to be the one to make her come. It sounded bad coming from my mouth, but it was true. I wanted to be the person to turn her on, the way she turned me on at her gig. She was my rock star; I in turn wanted to be her superhero. I didn't want Superman to be her superhero.

"So you don't want to use it on me?" she asked.

I nodded. "Is that okay?"

A pause hung in the air. I imagined her fucking Superman. I imagined her at a swingers' party with Spiderman and Aquaman and Daredevil and the Green Lantern, marveling at their giant fictional cocks.

"Okay, fine," she finally said, falling onto her pillow. "No dildo."

It was about dinnertime on a Friday a few weeks later. I went out for a beer with Gerard to ask him for advice.

Gerard had a big sexual history. When we drank, he would speak of Lucy So-and-So with the gorgeous eyes, and Jen What's-Her-Name with the perfect abs. He even had the dreamy, tired look of a guy who never has to masturbate. He had a scruffy beard; his hair was always messy. He always looked like he'd just come from a decent lay.

I asked him about the art of seduction.

"Ah, young grasshopper," he began, setting down his pint glass. "So you want to know how the master does it?"

"Yes," I said. "Yes, I do."

He proudly grinned and asked me some questions. He asked what turned me on. "Don't think, just say it, whatever it is."

I thought of all the porn clips I'd masturbated to and all the sexual fantasies I'd had. I thought of those videos my dad keeps in his sock drawer labeled TAXES.

"Come on, say it, Dave," he said. "What turns you on? Tell me!"

"The thought of Kelly coming," I said. I don't know where it had come from, but there it was. I imagined Kelly naked on my bed, moaning to the ceiling, bunching the bedsheets in her balled-up fists. I thought of her red-painted toes clenching. Then I thought of my tongue sliding up her thighs to her pussy. I wanted to taste her come, feel it spray into my mouth.

"Nice choice, champ," Gerard said, gulping his beer. "So you know what you've gotta do. You've gotta make her come."

I confided in him that we hadn't actually had sex yet. I told him all about the Superman dildo, and how it freaked me out. But Gerard didn't answer. He stood and walked over to the jukebox, pulled out a plastic bag of coins and put quarters into the machine. Chuck Berry's cover of the song "My Ding-a-Ling" burst into the air. Older people in the bar shot Gerard strange looks as he danced over to me, singing along with the insinuating lyrics about wanting to play with his ding-a-ling.

"Is this some kind of masturbation innuendo?" I asked. "Are you trying to imply something?"

"Just listen, man," he said, sitting back down. He struck the pose he always strikes when he's about to deliver a lecture. Or when he's about to ask a girl out. "This song is about a goddamn bell. But everybody seems to *think* it's all about dick. To me, this confusion raises an interesting discussion about sex."

I took a long sip of beer. "Interesting how?"

"I mean, what do you think sex is about? Is it about your ding-a-ling, or about *music?* Is it about the body, or the *harmony* of bodies?"

I stared at him blankly. I had no idea what he meant by sex being like music, but hearing the guitar riff play throughout the bar led me to think about Kelly, on the first night I'd laid eyes on her. She was radiant onstage, totally carefree, something that to me was unfamiliar and strange. I was dating a rock star. Is that what he meant by sex being like music?

I stood, leaving my pint glass half-empty.

"Gotta go," I said. I left Gerard enough to cover both of our drinks. I told him to consider it a payment for his services to the dating world.

"Thanks," Gerard said, smiling. "Remember: *music*."

I felt silly, but I knew what I had to do.

In my closet were several superhero shirts. Since I'd started dating Kelly, I tried not to wear them too often. I wanted to dress well for her. But this night was different. I pulled out my Superman T-shirt, fashioned a cape out of my red bath towel and left for her dorm room. It was only fair, after all. Kelly accepted all of my quirky passions, but I made her feel strange for wanting to use the Superman dildo.

This was my chance to right my wrongs. If I've learned anything from superheroes it's that they don't decide when and how they have to solve their problems; they just do what needs doing.

When I knocked on Kelly's door, she wasn't there. Her roommate answered the door, bursting out laughing. She had friends over, and they all laughed too, asking if I was off to rescue a cat out of a tree. I asked if they knew where Kelly had gone. They kept laughing, but when they finally wiped the tears from their eyes, they told me she'd gone to the beach.

The beach. Of course. Where she writes music.

"Thanks," I said, and dashed down the hall.

It was getting dark out; a few stars were visible overhead. I jogged to the beach in my costume. I heard laughter coming from the cars of students driving by. Many honked and yelled things, but I just ignored them and ran faster. I sprinted as I began to smell the sweet scent of the ocean.

Kelly was standing right where we'd gone on our very first date. She was staring out into the dark ocean.

"Kelly," I said. "Listen, I've been a dick."

She turned to face me. When she saw my costume, she burst out laughing. I laughed with her.

"You look ridiculous," she said. "But amazing, nonetheless."

She moved into my arms and I held her close. We kissed. We pressed our lips into each other's, nibbling on each other. I inhaled the smell of her, apologizing over and over again. I told her I was being insecure.

"You were jealous," she said. "You were jealous of Superman, weren't you?"

"Yes," I admitted. "I was jealous of Superman."

She laughed. Then we stripped off our clothes and ran into the water. We lay naked in the ocean-soaked sand. Kelly's skin was wet, framed by the moonlight. I put my lips to her chest, kissed between her breasts. I rubbed between her legs, pushing my fingers warmly inside. She closed her eyes and bit her lip.

Then I asked her to get the Superman dildo, and she trotted off to grab it. I watched her running naked, disappearing into the dark.

In that moment, I realized what Gerard meant about sex being like music. Sex is about listening. I had only been listening to *my* wants and desires.

When Kelly returned, she handed me the dildo and a tub of lube, and joined me on the blanket she spread on the sand. I held her legs open, letting her ankles rest on my shoulders.

"You're beautiful," I said in a heavy breath. "You deserve to hear that every day."

"I always knew Superman had charm," she said, rolling her eyes.

I rubbed a dollop of lube onto her pussy, feeling her moisten with pleasure. I slid the Superman dildo deeply inside of her and rubbed her clit. She grabbed me, pulled our bodies close together and dug her nails into my back.

"Please go faster," she said.

I moved the dildo as fast I could. Kelly squeezed her thighs around my arm. "Oh, Dave." Hearing her say my name made it clear to me: she didn't want Superman—or at least, not only Superman—she wanted *me*. She grabbed my dick tightly, giving as good as she got. The music metaphor was exactly right: the surging energy of our bodies rocketed to our own beautiful rhythm. This was even better than my fantasies. Kelly moaned to the burning stars, slapping her clitoris until she squirted onto the dildo.

I lay on top of her and listened to the beat of her heart. I'd never felt more alive. We laughed and screamed all night while the waves of the Atlantic tried to hush us. But they couldn't.

Nothing could ever hush us.

LOST AND POUNDED

Zee Giovanni

The selection seemed endless. Rope toys, chew toys, toys to chase around. I looked at the little black dog pacing at my feet.

"How do you choose one?" I asked her. She wagged her tail. The blank, happy expression on her face told me nothing.

"Need some help?"

The man walking toward me wore a dress shirt, slacks and suspenders, not the bright blue polo of the pet supply store employees. He was short and stocky, but I could detect a hint of muscle bulging from his dark skin. I thought he was trans but didn't want to assume how he identified. He had a warm, easy smile as he approached, and I didn't miss the approving glance he gave my cleavage as he adjusted the bag over his shoulder and the folder under his arm. The dog at my feet leapt forward, standing on her hind paws at the edge of the leash when he reached us.

"You don't look like you work here," I pointed out, pulling

the dog back so she wouldn't jump all over this stranger. The observation was true, and commenting on his appearance gave me a good excuse to stare lustfully at his body a little longer.

"I don't," the man said. He gestured at his bag. "But I'm something of an expert in toys. It's kind of what I do."

I nodded, understanding the outfit now. He must be some kind of sales rep. My arms began to ache under the surprising strength of the little dog straining against them. She whined and ran her spindly legs in place on the floor.

"Can I pet her?" he asked.

"Please do," I said. "I've never seen her so excited to see someone."

The man knelt down and brought his face close to the dog's as he rubbed her back. They looked like a good match—short legs, tight black curls atop their heads. It was sweet.

"What's her name?"

I hesitated. "Lulu?"

I didn't mean for it to sound more like a question than a statement, but it did. The truth was that I had no idea what the dog's name was, because she wasn't mine. Just an hour earlier, I'd found her trotting about the yard in front of my building. I knew I couldn't keep her, but only a week had passed since my girlfriend Allison dumped me for another woman, and to say I was feeling lonely would be the understatement of the year. The dog and I could spend a harmless afternoon keeping each other company, I reasoned. And then I could get to work on finding her owner.

But this stranger didn't need to know the details. I appreciated the attention he was giving my long legs as he petted the dog, and I didn't want to throw his admiration off with my ethically questionable behavior.

"And what's your name?" he asked, standing up.

"Flo. And yours?"

"I'm Arroc. You can call me Roc."

Roc reached for a blue stuffed bunny and Lulu perked up, her tail wagging even more rapidly. He squeezed it, and a chirp escaped from its center.

"I'd suggest this one for Lulu," he said. "Seems like she'd enjoy something that squeaks. And for you, Flo, I'd suggest we go someplace more private and see what you might like in my bag."

I looked at the bulging bag, and then back at Roc. His deep brown eyes were fixed steadily on mine, searching for a reaction.

"Are we still talking about dog toys?" I asked.

Roc laughed. "No. I have to admit, you've got my mind wandering elsewhere."

He tossed the toy to Lulu, who attacked it enthusiastically, making the squeaker cry out. It looked like that would keep her busy for a while. His smile was irresistible, so I didn't even try to hold back.

"Let's go see what you've got," I said.

I drove us back to my place, chatting with Roc as Lulu napped comfortably in his lap, worn out from her spurt of energy in the store. We went right into what we wanted to share before hooking up, rattling off the details of our lives like stats printed on baseball cards.

"I had a girlfriend. Two years. Dumped me last week," I said.

"Ouch," Roc said. "Fresh wounds, huh?"

"Yeah. I'm feeling the need to lick them."

I settled into the drive, feeling more comfortable with him now that he knew what to expect—Allison's belongings still littering my apartment. He told me about his transition from female to male, which began about two years ago.

"I also had a girlfriend. Five years. Left when I started the hormones. Said she didn't sign up to be with a man."

"I'm sorry," I said.

He shrugged. "It was the first time she acknowledged me as a man, so I already knew we didn't fit. I took it as a compliment at the time."

By the time we reached my apartment, we'd had enough conversation. Roc dropped his bag and his folder and I dropped Lulu's leash and spread my hands over the canvas of his back like he was a new art project. He put his fingers in my Afro and tugged me toward him, meeting my mouth with his and electrifying my body with his dexterous tongue. I took his hands and pulled him into the bedroom, not wanting to spoil the moment by tripping over Allison's boxes near the door or knocking down one of our happy couple photos still adorning the living room walls. I'd been longing to forget about Allison for even a minute, and I had a feeling Roc could give me plenty of time to do just that. He picked up his bag and followed me down the hall.

"I want to show you something," he said, tossing his things onto the bed.

The bag unzipped with a throaty groan, and I nearly repeated the sound when Roc bent over my bed, his body all at once doughy and firm in just the right places. He was pulling items from the bag, and he'd spread almost all of them out before I wrenched my eyes from his body to see what he had.

"This is what I do," he said, and I thought back to when he'd called himself "something of an expert in toys."

What an expert he was. He had with him harnesses, vibrators and dildos, of so many various sizes that my pussy contracted and released all on its own as I imagined each inside me.

"You sell these?" I asked.

"Yep," he said, puffing his chest proudly. "I've learned to turn one of my greatest passions into a job skill. I've got quite a bit to say about every one of these, so I can put my experience to good use to make sales."

I didn't need him to say a thing. I just wanted him to show me what he could do. I stepped closer, wriggling out of my jeans as I approached the bed. His eyes caressed my hips and ass while I looked at the toys, licking my lips as I struggled to decide which would be most delicious.

Roc stepped behind me, pushed himself against my ass and brought his hands up my shirt to encircle my nipples. His breath warmed my neck, and his lips lapped at my earlobe as he spoke.

"Lady's choice," he said. "Pick one."

I giggled like a girl in a jewelry store. Allison had never been fond of toys, so I hadn't played with them much recently, and now I had so many to choose from. Though they all looked delectable, I was drawn most to the thick dildos that reminded me of Roc's skin, brown rubber rippled and darkened in lines like human veins. I picked up the largest of those, surprising even myself, as I wasn't even sure if I could take it all in my pussy. I felt Roc's chest heave with a deep breath as I lifted it into the air.

"That one?" he said. He reached for a leather harness. "Do you want this, too?"

I sure did. I nodded, brushing my thick hair across his face and down his chest. He stepped away from me, taking the chosen items aside and shoving the rest back in the bag. I took my panties off, climbed on the bed and touched my clit while I watched him undress and assemble the strap-on. He'd been packing beneath his pants already, and he set that piece aside.

The possibility that I could've grabbed his cock right there in the store made my clit jump. His sturdy thighs were plush with the leather clinging to them. His expert hands fastened every buckle quickly before resting on his hips to display the large, succulent dick standing upright toward me. He watched my fingers fly over my glistening pussy. I paused and spread my pussy lips with my fingers, inviting him in.

He was on me in a flash, coaxing my fingers aside to feel my cunt for himself. His nimble fingers danced inside me, while his tongue played the same rhythm on my nipples beneath my shirt, making them point rigidly to the sky. Then his lips climbed my neck, pausing in front of my mouth to ask a question.

"May I pull your hair?"

I laughed at the simultaneous politeness and crassness of the question, delivered with his cock resting on my thigh and his fingers inside my dripping cunt.

"Yes, you may," I said.

The swiftness of what happened next assailed me, and I gasped as Roc switched from courteous gentleman to powerful daddy, from asking permission to taking me for himself. He gripped a large puff of my hair in his fist and dragged me up against the headboard. He kept my head under his control as he brought his cock up to my lips.

"Open up," he said, gently but firmly.

I took a deep breath and obeyed, my body tingling with surprise, uncertainty and desire. The head of his cock widened my lips, and then the rest followed. At first, I gagged on the shaft, saliva spilling down my chin from my gurgling throat. It had been a while since I'd sucked dick, and I'd never tried to suck one this big before. Roc let me take my time, but he was unyielding, determined to get his cock down my throat. I remembered my old tricks, found a steady breathing pattern and pushed my head forward, deep-throating the dildo. I couldn't take it all, but I looked up to see that I'd taken enough to make Roc smile.

"That's right, suck that dick," he said.

He kept repeating those words, *that's right,* and I felt so happy to please him, I purred, shaking his dick in my trembling mouth. He pulled out of my mouth and stroked his slick cock while he watched me take off my shirt and bra. I slid back down the bed. I was happy to be under his power, to do what he wanted, but I wanted some, too, emboldened by the triumph of taking the dildo in my mouth. Now, I wanted to see what my pussy could do.

Roc brought his dick to my pussy lips and looked up to my eyes, as if to ask permission once more. I'm sure my plump lips formed a perfect O on my face, as I was both terrified and thrilled to take his massive dick inside me. I nodded, and he entered my pussy just as he'd entered my mouth, gradually but insistently. The stiff rubber opened me up as it penetrated me, and each time I thought it was all I could take, Roc showed me he had more to give, filling me up deeply and generously.

I moaned and moaned. This time, Roc wasn't holding me in his grip, but I was still under his power, held captive by the enormous dick taking root within me. He began to buck, and I thought he might open my pussy with an eruption like I'd never felt before, giving me nothing to do but hold on, seizing the bedspread in my hands and arching my back to take him in as deeply as possible. The leather of his harness slapped against my skin to let me know that each thrust had gone all the way in.

I don't know if it was the scent of the leather mixing with the musk of our desire, or the blissful pain of his rocking inside me, but something had me feeling light-headed. My neck rolled around like I was intoxicated, drunk with glee. Roc had me floating away to a heavenly place, and though we were talking, I felt no control over my own voice.

"Take my dick. Tell me how you like it," he said.

"Oh, I like your big dick deep inside me."

"You really like it?"

"Oh, I *really* like it. Oh, Roc, I'm gonna come on your dick."

Hearing that, Roc picked up his pace, lifting my legs into the air and hammering into me with hard, heavy thrusts. An orgasm rippled through me, and he held my legs on his chest and kissed them as they jerked. My moans felt like sobs in the way they released my emotions, shaking loose something I'd been holding tightly inside and allowing me to submit to all the pleasure he pumped into me.

Slowly, Roc pulled out of my pussy, admiring the juices dripping from his dick as he did. He nestled beside me, kissing my shoulders and running his soft hands up and down my body. We both breathed heavily into the bedspread.

After a few moments, I stood up slowly, unsure of myself. I found my footing and ambled gingerly into the hall. Grateful for what Roc had delivered, I suddenly remembered my manners as host to a houseguest.

"I'll get us some water," I said.

In the kitchen, Lulu came trotting up to me, and I bent down to pat her. I noticed that papers had fallen out of Roc's folder when he dropped it by the door, so I gathered them up to make sure he didn't lose them. I was already thirsty, but my mouth felt parched as soon as I noticed what was printed on the posters: a photo of Lulu, along with an offer of a reward for her safe return and a number to call. I shook my head, sank down on the couch, and grabbed my cell phone. I dialed the number on the poster, and heard ringing from the bedroom. Roc's voice echoed through the phone and down the hall.

"Hello?"

"I wasn't going to keep her," I said.

"I know."

"How could you know?"

"Not sure. I just felt I could trust you. And besides, at least if you stole her, I knew she'd been in good hands." His laugh filled both my ears.

"What's her name?" I asked.

"Trixie."

"Trixie," I repeated. The dog hopped to me, wagging her tail. For some reason, she trusted me, too.

"Come back in here," Roc said.

I shook my head, even though he couldn't see me. "No. I'm too embarrassed."

"Would you feel better if I punished you for what you've done?"

The sound of Roc's unzipping bag ripped through the apartment. A shiver whipped through me.

"I'd like that," I said. "Though the poster says I should get a reward."

"I'll give you that, too."

I hung up the phone and bounced back into the bedroom, but not before giving that little black dog a big kiss on the head for the joy she'd brought me.

IN THE PINK

Rob Rosen

F uck!" I cursed, slamming the car door behind me. "Forgot
the fucking contract."

Which was fairly ironic, seeing as the reason I'd been working
late, the reason I suddenly found myself with a weekend full of
paperwork instead of a weekend full of sun and fun was because
of said contract.

"Fuck," I cursed. And, yes, it bore repeating—loudly.

And so I tromped back inside the building, echoing the word
over and over again, even as I entered the elevator, as I unlocked
the office and as I trudged back to my desk. Though it was
amended barely a split second later, two more words promptly
tacked on.

"What the fuck?"

See, though the office was dark, all the desks evacuated, not
a peep to be heard, there was a light coming from the supply
closet, errant beams shining through from the bottom crack.
Since I'd been the last person in the supply closet—inside the

office for that matter, as far as I knew—and since I was certain I'd flicked the light off upon my departure, the "what the" added to the "fuck" seemed well merited.

Which is why I found myself tiptoeing to the closet door, thick contract gripped beneath my armpit, heart rate suddenly ramping up to a six on the Richter, seven as I silently gripped the knob, eight as I flung the door wide open.

"What the fuck?" I shouted. "What the fuck? What the fuck? What the fuck?"

Again it bore repeating, except now for wholly and again well-merited reason.

With my heart now pounding a good solid ten, I dropped the contract and tore away from the closet, face so red that molten lava would pale in comparison.

"Josh, wait!" I heard, barely a moment later. "Wait, please!"

I didn't wait, though. Not until I felt his hand on my shoulder. "I didn't see anything," I blurted out, my back to his front, the sound of heavy breathing, both his and mine, filling the otherwise stone-cold silent office.

"I can explain," he replied, his voice as wobbly and shaky as my knees suddenly were.

Slowly I turned, shoulders bunched up, eyes in a squint. For there he stood, naked, save for my contract covering his privates, hairy chest rapidly expanding and contracting. "I'd, um, rather you didn't, Pete," I told him. "Explain, that is."

Now, to be fair, I'd only ever seen my coworker in a suit and tie before. Suffice it to say, the image of him in the closet, naked and spread-eagle, fucking himself with lord only knew what, would forever be burnished in my memory. So, yeah, I really didn't need or want an explanation as to what he'd been doing.

He handed me the contract. I stared down. For some odd

reason, his cock was still mostly turgid. And, fine, it was a nice cock, as cocks went, but it was Pete's, my coworker's, so I tried, again mostly, to look away. "It's my wife's fault," he blurted out.

I stood frozen to the spot as I fought to hold back a nervous chuckle. Two seconds later, it was chuckle, one, Josh, zero. "It's your wife's fault that you're alone in the office at night, naked and, uh..." I pointed downward. He, or that is to say, *it* was pointing up.

"Fucking myself?" he said, thereby finishing my train of thought.

I nodded. "Yeah, that."

He forced a grin onto his sweat-soaked face. Surprisingly, he then moved his hand from his front to his back. I heard the audible *pop* first, his eyelids momentarily fluttering as he retrieved the pink, portable prick from his port side, a grunt then added to his repertoire.

I grunted in sync with him. The dildo was on the large side. Sucker looked mighty painful in fact. Also explained why his prick was still thick, I supposed.

"You're gay, Josh, right?"

Again I chuckled. "Odd segue, Pete."

He blushed, though, all things considered, it seemed a bit late on his part. "I mean, you're, well, accustomed to, um, uh..."

I lifted my hand up for him to please stop. "Are we really going to have this conversation, Pete? Couldn't we just forget that I saw all this?" Which was about like asking Pearl Harbor to forget that it'd been bombed.

He nodded. "It's just that, my wife, Janet, see, she let me, well...*fuck her* last week." He rolled his hands in the air and glanced away. "Up the, uh, well, *you know.*" I squirmed. I had, after all, met Janet before. And the image of her getting her ass worked over wasn't a pretty one. "Now she wants to return the favor." With his free hand, the one not holding the quivering dildo, he was pointing to his rump.

My hand was still held up in the cease-and-desist mode. I lowered it. "So you were simply practicing?" I dreaded asking the question, but curiosity suddenly had my cat in a stranglehold.

He nodded. "Not like I could do it at home, with her there, I mean."

I too nodded, though his logic seemed less than solid. "Got it." I turned to leave. "And, um, good luck with, uh, *everything*." I pointed at the fake dick still held firmly in his grip.

"Wait!" he shouted, yet again.

I sighed as I shook the contract his way. "Pete," I said, "it's been...*fun*, but I have a load of work to do. Really."

He sighed as he shook the dildo my way. "I can help. Give me half of it to work on."

I knew better than to think he was being altruistic. "In exchange for what? My silence? Done. Don't even give it a second thought." Unlike me, who would surely have tenths and twentieths.

"Not your silence, no."

I paused. "Then what?"

It was now his turn to pause, one of the pregnant variety, and nine months pregnant at that. "It's just...I'm not finding it...well...*enjoyable*."

I pointed from the real prick to the fake one. "I think you went too big, comparatively speaking."

"It's the wife's."

I stifled a grin. "Oh."

He nodded. "Yeah, *oh*. In any case, I don't think I'm doing it right."

I scratched my head. "You stick it in. You fuck your ass. You jack off, Pete," I told him, truly wishing that this conversation was done with. Mostly. "Not rocket science."

His nodding went into overdrive. "It's just sort of hard to, well, fuck and jack at the same time."

I gulped. "Please tell me you're not about to ask me what I think you're about to ask me, Pete."

His nodding abruptly stopped, the red again working its way up his neck. "In exchange for half your workload."

"Uh-huh. So let me get this, for lack of a better word, *straight*," the gay guy, namely me, said. "You want me to fuck your ass, in the office, to prep you for your wife?"

The nodding returned. "Fuck me with the dildo, Josh," he said. "Nothing, um, *physical* of course."

"Of course." I looked down at my thick contract and then down at his thick prick. Sadly, the contract was thicker. Sadly for me, that is. And maybe a bit for Janet. "You sure about this, Pete? I mean, you and me have never even had lunch together. Now you want me to fuck you—"

"With the dildo," he interrupted.

"Right," I said. "With the dildo. And, again, you sure that's such a wise idea?"

He shrugged. "Look, you've already seen me naked."

"And then some," I couldn't help but add.

"Exactly," he agreed. "Might as well get something out of it. Like half your weekend back."

And untold years of uncomfortable office meetings in our future, I thought. In any case, he was right; I had already seen him naked, exposed. In other words, in for a penny, in for a pound. Though, looking at the dildo, pound*ing* was more like it. And so I handed him half the contract. "Better be thorough," I cautioned him.

He forced a smile. "I believe I can say the same thing." The dildo moved from his hand to mine. "And please be gentle."

Good luck with that. "I'll do my best, Pete."

So back to the supply closet we went. Odd to say, yes, but in the grand scheme of things, namely that I found myself staring down at my coworker's bare, hairy ass, not all that odd. He'd put a leather seat inside, I soon found, a towel draped across it, a bottle of lube set on the floor. The scene looked both obscene and sterile. I'd never look at it or him the same way again, of that I was certain.

He hopped in the chair and looked up at me, hope in his eyes. I stared down at him. Guy was at least nice looking, toned and hairy, so things could've been worse. He then lifted his legs and spread them, his pink, puckered hole winking my way. I gulped as I stared at the dildo in my hand. It swayed—which made two of us. Three if you included the chair, which shook and rocked as he positioned and repositioned himself.

"No wonder it was unenjoyable, Pete," I told him. "A chair in a supply closet is not exactly comfortable."

He shrugged. "The floor is dirty."

I grinned. "Gee, is that your biggest concern here?"

The shrug amped up. "Just fuck me already, okay?"

My grin matched his shrug. "Not what I expected to hear when I came to work today."

In any case, I crouched down, face to ass. So, yeah, also not what I expected to *see* today either. In any case, I lifted the bottle of lube and coated the dildo with it. Thankfully, he didn't complain when I did the same to his tight little hair-rimmed hole. He also didn't complain when I released my beast and gave it a tug. *I mean, why should he have all the fun?* I figured.

Again I stared up. Josh was stroking his pole, heavy balls bouncing, cock growing thicker by the second—his and mine both. Go figure. I placed the head of the pink appendage against his tender chute. Slowly, gently, I slid barely the head inside. He sucked in his breath, the stroke on his prick going still. I waited for him to relax.

"You okay?" I asked.

He nodded. "Just go slowly."

"No prob." And so slowly I went, teasing it inside of him, teasing it outside, in and out, slow and steady, until his cock was finally at full mast. "Better?"

He grunted, then groaned, then exhaled sharply. "I'm beginning to see what all the fuss is about," he panted in reply, as the pace of his hand's movements on his thick prick quickened. I matched him, stroke for stroke. Maybe we'd come together. Very romantic. I grinned at the thought, a full-on smile then stretching wide across my face as I finally managed to get the length and breadth and width of that phallic wonder up his tight tush.

Suddenly, Pete was groaning with abandon, especially once I piston-fucked his hole with gusto. As for that office chair, it was groaning with abandon as well. Never one to be left out, I joined the happy pair.

"Fuck!" he soon wailed. "Fuck, fuck, fuck." His ass was now off the seat, balls ricocheting this way and that.

He was close. I was closer. I stood up and pounded his amply stretched hole. His eyes were closed, his mouth in a pant, cock but a blur as he coaxed the come up. Me, I was furiously stroking as well, a torrent of sweat pouring down my face.

"Do it," I croaked out, my legs starting to buckle.

"*Fuuuck*," he groaned one final time, his back arched, head tilted in reverse.

The dildo was buried to the hilt as his cock at last erupted. Sucker was super thick now. Still not as thick as my contract, but still. I moaned as I watched him shoot and shoot and shoot, come flinging up before raining down on his hairy belly. At the sight of it, the sound, the smell, my own cock throbbed and promptly shot, the creamy mess splashing across his left thigh, a thick band dripping down his hairy nut-sac. Pretty, yes. Pretty weird, also yes.

"Well?" I asked him, waiting for the postcoital glow to fade.

He popped his eyes open. "Did I already say *fuck*?"

I nodded. "Repeatedly."

"Do you think my wife enjoyed it that much?"

My nodding abruptly stopped. "Seems doubtful." He laughed, come dripping down to the floor below. Dirty, like he'd said. Only more so. "We, uh, *good* now?"

He pointed past his withering tool. "One more thing."

I grinned as I gently eased the pink peter from his ass. The now-familiar *pop* quickly ensued. He sighed as his hole was again free of it. I sighed as I handed it back to him. "Well, good luck with Janet then."

"Thanks," he said, running his index finger through the sticky, gooey, aromatic mess.

"Don't mention it," I said, turning to leave as I stuffed my prick back inside my slacks.

Seriously, don't. Not ever. And, please, dear god, not to your wife.

Still, as I stared down at the much thinner contract, I smiled. After all, I'd certainly done my part for gay/straight relations, not to mention office morale. In other words, unlike how I'd previously left the office that night, I now found myself, well, *in the pink*, so to speak. And I certainly wasn't cursing my luck this time around.

DALIA'S TOY

Corrine A. Silver

I only had a poker night once every few months, inviting the guys over after all our little ones were in bed. They were a good group, guys I worked with or knew from the neighborhood. We played in the garage, smoking cigars and drinking pretentious craft-brewed beer. The baby monitor was clipped to my belt, but I was lucky—my son, Ian, was a good sleeper.

Dalia always went out with her girlfriends on my poker nights. Admittedly, most of her girlfriends were my friends' wives, but they almost never went out at night. They were "ladies who lunched," friends from the playground, trading recipes and parenting tips. Nights were for family, weekends for church and seeing the in-laws.

The game wasn't anything unusual. I finished a little behind breaking even, and the guys stayed to finish their cigars and beers. We shot the shit, the way guys do, talking without really saying anything. Talking shit about who we'd fuck if we were single, about our bosses, about the annoying neighbor—whatever. After they were gone, I started cleaning up the garage, but Dalia called and I paused to answer my cell.

"Hey, baby. What's up? You okay?" All the shit-talking jackassery had left my voice because she was my weakest weak spot.

Loud club music thumped in the distance and, even though she was yelling into the phone, her words were slurred a little. "Hey, hon! No...No, yeah, I'm okay. Better than okay! Having so much fun."

I smiled at the excitement in her voice, even as my curiosity was piqued—my proper woman didn't get drunk anymore. I could imagine her face, flushed from dancing or wine or both, eyes too bright. Right when I was about to ask her what was up again, I heard her muffling the phone as she spoke to someone else. "I know! Fuck off, Ginger! I'm not a pussy."

Ginger was one of her friends from the Daughters of the Revolution chapter in town, and my friend Keith's wife. She was very similar to Dalia: proper. But I heard loud yelling and laughing and then Dalia was back on the phone.

"Hey, Eric?"

I laughed. "Yeah, honey?"

"There's a sex toy store around the corner from this bar and the girls dared me to go get something. So...I'm gonna do it. I just didn't want you to be freaked out when you saw the charge on the card." She was still giggling, but I couldn't speak for a moment.

My sweet, pure wife, in a sex shop?

"Eric?"

I jolted back to the conversation. "Yeah, okay, hon. That's cool. Have fun."

Her voice got quieter, huskier. "Anything you want me to get?"

She was booze brave and it gave me a hard-on.

I smiled indulgently even though she couldn't see it. "You get whatever you want, baby girl." I probably hadn't called her that since before Ian was born.

"Okay, boo." She was slurring her words enough that I worried some.

"But hey—how are you girls getting home? Do you have a designated driver?"

"No, but there's a guy here who said he'd drive us."

"*What?*"

I was nearly deafened by the laughter. "I'm kidding! Shit, lighten up! No, we took a cab from Ginger and Keith's place. I'll call you if I can't drive when we get back there. Shouldn't be too much longer."

"Jesus. Okay, honey, Keith just left, so have him drive you home if you're still messed up. I'm sure he wouldn't mind." I caught myself before I launched into a whole talk about safety that hadn't been an issue since we graduated college. "Just be careful. See you in a bit."

I finished cleaning up, but then I couldn't decide what to do with myself. I felt excited in a way that I hadn't been in a long time. Just because it was different, a change from the norm in our house. Dalia wasn't a prude, per se. She was just…conservative, self-critical, inhibited. I cringed at the honest assessment of my wife. She was a lot of other things as well. Smart, kind, loving. An amazing mother. Supportive of me all through medical school and residency. Just not really sexually adventurous.

I grabbed another beer from the fridge and sat on the couch to watch ESPN until she got home, nervously checking my phone every two or three minutes. The waiting was ridiculous. I wasn't getting anything out of watching TV, just thinking of her steeling her spine to walk into some sleazy sex shop. I knew her, knew she'd feel all the shame in the world, but would walk in with her head held high.

I mumbled to myself, "I'll wait another ten minutes before calling her."

But it didn't matter; she called me to tell me she was on her way home from Ginger and Keith's place. She was still laughing a bunch, but her words were clearer.

About fifteen minutes later, she came in. And the first thing that hit me was how much she looked like she did in college at the end of a frat party. Hair flat, face shiny and flushed. Mascara smudged under her eyes. Wide, funny smile on her face.

I stood as she entered the room. "Hey, baby girl." I smiled at her, but let her come to me.

"Hi." She smiled wide and teetered her way over to me. "I got us a new toy." She fell into giggles again as a flush infused her cheeks.

"Yeah?" I pulled her to me with an arm around her waist. "Well, what is it?"

She twisted away from me. "Come on—I'll show you."

She pulled my hand, but in the opposite direction from the stairs up to our bedroom. Instead, she pulled me down to the basement. Her little plastic shopping bag slapped against her leg, jostling the stuff inside. It seemed like there was more than one thing in there.

I let her pull me along and at the bottom of the stairs, she turned to me abruptly. "Okay. Ready?"

"Sure."

Now...I watch porn sometimes. I kind of felt like I knew what to expect; the only thing that would be surprising would be that it was *my Dalia* holding whatever she pulled out of the bag.

I was wrong. The baggie she pulled out just looked like it was full of bright crimson puppet fur. I cocked my head to the side, about to ask, but she cut me off by pulling another package out. This one was a deep blue circle about the diameter of a golf ball, but it had a small dolphin attached to one side of it.

When I looked back up at her face, something was different. Her angelic face was *devious*. Her voice was low and husky when she said, "Come over here, Eric."

She walked farther into the basement and reached back for my hand. I gave it to her without speaking, just watching her. She went deep into the room, past the play area cluttered with toys, past the TV, almost to the laundry room. She turned back to me and her eyes were heavy-lidded, like she was getting sleepy, but her lips were spread in a small dirty smile.

"Let's get you naked." She murmured the words and dropped her purse and the cheap, plastic bag from her hands to reach for my belt.

I watched her hands and when I reached to help her, she slapped me away. She pulled my pants down and squatted at my feet to help me step out of them, but instead of standing up, she stayed there and reached for my boxers. I pulled my polo over my head and she pulled at my shorts, negotiating them over my cock. I was hard. Hard before she even touched me. Hard before I even saw her naked. I'd been half-hard since her call from the bar.

She still didn't stand. She just ran her fingertips over my dick, like it was the first time she had ever seen it. Her touch was light, and when she lightly dragged her nails over the sensitive skin of the head, a chill chased over my skin.

"Okay, come down here." She glanced up at me and I knelt on the floor, reaching for her. She smiled and shook her head. "No. Lie down."

I did and she stood, just next to my arm, and reached under her skirt to pull her thong off. I got just a glimpse of her skin as she moved. She walked past my head and then dropped down to her knees. "Give me your hands."

I arched my neck so I could look back at her even as I moved to give her my hands. She had the furry thing out and was looping it around the foot of the big heavy sofa. And then she was looping it in on itself. It was a soft restraint—sort of fluffy fabric cuffs. She pulled each of my hands into one of the loops she had made and then she tightened them down.

When she looked back at my face, there was a glint in her eyes that gave me a moment of pause. It reminded me of the look on her face when she had decided that our garden was going to be better than Tessi Newbottom's across the street.

She crawled over me and put my cock in her mouth, completely obliterating Tessi Newbottom from my thoughts. Dalia's lips were hot and wet as she licked at me clumsily. She didn't normally suck my dick. She'd said she didn't like it, had never liked it, but she sure seemed to like it in that moment.

When I started locking my legs and arching my hips up at her, she paused to say, "Okay, now for this."

She wrestled the dolphin ring out of its package and stretched it. It was some kind of elastic rubber material. She slipped it around the head of my cock and shimmied it down to the base. It was snug without being tight, but triggered a whole new awareness of my cock. I got harder.

She swiped a finger across my tip, smearing a bit of precome around the sensitive skin there. I gasped. Dalia glanced up at my face like she had just remembered I was there. Her eyes were still half-mast, her lips were parted just a bit, lipstick smeared, lips almost bruised looking. I could see her tongue, just brushing the back of her teeth.

A look of blank, empty need crossed her face and she threw her leg over me, straddling me, the head of my cock just nudging her. And she was *wet*. Soaked. Drenched. I flicked my eyes back to hers, about to voice my pleasured shock, when I saw a shadow of my prim and proper wife there. There was a shade of insecurity.

So I said nothing. Just waited to see what she would do. And while she held my gaze, her face settled some. The insecurity was gone and she let the tension out of her thighs to glide onto me. I moaned low and tight in my chest. Because it was hot as fuck watching her. Because she was the least inhibited I had ever seen her. Because she still had her dress on and I was naked, tied up underneath her.

But then she cocked her hips and pushed me into her deeper. She moaned so low in her throat that it almost sounded like pain. She reached between us and grabbed the ring of rubber on my cock. She fiddled with it for a minute before I felt it give, then start buzzing.

Now she rolled her hips in a circle and closed her eyes, moaning each time her clit hit the nose of the little buzzing dolphin.

"Baby girl, I want to touch you." Her eyes were wide and guileless, and for a moment she didn't react at all. Slowly, devious mischief crept across her features, ending with a smart-ass smirk on her lips.

"No. Tonight, you're my toy. And a toy doesn't move unless I move it." Her voice was so hard, but her pussy was clamping and releasing my cock. I sucked in a tight breath.

"Okay, Dalia. I'm your toy." I considered it, considered her for a moment. "So play with me."

She smiled softly and started flipping her hips over me, on me, grinding down into me at the deepest point in each thrust. I felt my muscles tighten and I wanted to pull against the restraint holding me stretched out for her. She didn't care. She just wanted to ride me.

"Come on. Let me see you. Take that damn dress off." I felt my rising testosterone making my voice gravelly.

She started to move, just a twitch, but her eyes flicked back to mine, and caught there. She giggled, but the devil in her expression gave me pause. This was a totally new side to my usually meek Dalia—and I liked it.

When I opened my mouth to speak, she slapped my face. Not too hard, just stinging, but it made my dick tighten and bulge, driving up into her. She felt it and watched me with a new level of curiosity, eyes glittering.

She leaned forward, planting her hands on either side of my chest. Her lips brushed over mine and she whispered, "Did you like that?"

I didn't answer her, just planted my feet and thrust up at her.

"Yes, just like that, toy." So I drove into her again and again, until she got twitchy and her breathing shuddered between us, whispered slick like sibilant turbulence. Her slickness coated my cock, slippery and warm, and that damn dolphin buzzed a low tingle, thrumming through my cock.

When I thought she was about to come, she leaned back, resting against my thighs, and just rolled her hips around on me. I let out a loud grunt of frustration and she gave me "the look." The you-can't-have-a-bowl-of-ice-cream-right-before-bed look. That look that says, *Stop whining. Your life is pretty damn good.*

Without speaking, she scraped her fingernails down my torso, leaving hot, red scratches. With a hand almost underneath herself, she grasped the base of my cock, over the ring, and started stroking it up and down, grinding the vibrating dolphin onto her clit, but making me goddamn crazy.

"Let me see your tits." She just glanced up at me, but then closed her eyes without answering. "Fuck! Come on, Dalia. You're killing me here!"

But a hot red flush was creeping up her neck and her collarbone glistened with sweat when she threw her head back, moaning like something wild. She ground her pelvis on mine, lost in sensation, so close to coming. A long, low growl moaned out of her chest as I felt her pussy tighten on me. She was so fucking close and I wanted to push her over the edge. I wanted to make her feel something so strong it scared her. I wanted her overwhelmed.

So I pushed at her with my hips even harder, until I arched up off the floor and her knees left the ground. Her eyes ratcheted open and met mine. I knew my smile was evil. I knew it because I felt it. I felt vicious and evil. It felt like the basest part of my brain was choosing for me and I liked it.

I let the tension out of my legs and flopped back onto the ground. She slumped down on top of me and the little cock ring vibrator slammed against her.

"Oh *fuck!*" She came hard, her cunt tightening and tightening, slick and liquid around me. And then she started shaking, and her tight pussy jiggled on me. She bit her lip and looked at me, yanking the front of her dress down so that her tits popped out. She clutched at her breasts, moaning, "Yeah, Eric, fuck me like a good toy."

It was too much—tied up with her on top, panting and acting like someone completely free of her usual hang-ups. My mouth watered and I started snapping my hips up against her. She rolled with it, accenting my thrusts, punctuating them with little yelps each time the dolphin tickled her. I only felt my orgasm building a moment before it fired. It was a thing completely beyond my control: fierce, wild and primal.

I came like a caveman, head thrown back, howling until she laughed and clamped her hand over my mouth, murmuring, "Shhhh, you'll wake the baby."

I silenced myself, but still shuddered against her until she rolled off me, laughing as she flopped onto the floor next to me. "I love you, Eric."

I twisted toward her. "I love you too, baby girl." I gave her a wry look. "Think you could untie me, now?"

When we got ready for bed that night, I saw the little bit of self-doubt creeping back into her, the shame at her own pleasure. I hated it. I wrapped my arms around her from behind as she looked in the mirror. I let my lips drift over her shoulder, her neck.

"Do you know how sexy you are?" She inhaled tightly, but I kept speaking before she could answer me. "You are beautiful and kind and sexy as hell. I loved seeing you like that. Free, just so fucking juicy."

She smiled and met my eyes in the mirror, flirting back. "You liked that, did you, toy?" And she pushed her ass back against my rehardening cock.

VEGETABLE LOVE

Susan St. Aubin

It begins in the supermarket, in the produce section, where I fondle carrots, celery, cucumbers, perhaps a winter pear with its narrow top widening to a sturdy base. Remove the stem and it's perfectly smooth, hard, not yet ripe, a young maiden of a pear. The celery, no, too narrow, too rough, but I might get it for soup, along with some onions. I put a wide, firm cucumber in my basket, then a bunch of long, hard carrots, and, so as not to arouse suspicion, hothouse tomatoes, lettuce and spinach for a salad. Too bad grapes aren't in season, but here are some imported cherries—expensive, but they might do. And from the butcher, a long, narrow soup bone, a perfect fit for me and my soup pot.

At my age I don't have the time or inclination to be anyone's coy mistress, so I take matters into my own hands. The long-haired man who selects only locally grown fruits and vegetables; the woman pushing a baby in a cart so full I can't see beyond the pack of disposable diapers on top; the bald man buying whiskey and bread and peanut butter—would they be shocked if they knew what this sweet grandmother was up to? Would they be hurt to learn that today I'm not interested in taking the time to meet them, embrace them or cook for them? No, my groceries are for myself and I want them now, before they decay. I load my finds into my car and drive fast, as if carried by wings along empty afternoon streets. This time is mine.

At home I scrub the pear, the cucumber and the cherries, removing stems and bumps, then peel a couple of carrots, soaking them all in a basin of warm water. Time becomes elastic, both speeding and slowing. I start with a long soak in a hot bath filled with chopped rosemary and lavender from my yard, remembering years of past lovers on whom I once depended for my pleasure. Some are gone for good while others have left me on my own, where I can race time or make it stand still, with no one to please but myself.

I have a particular fondness for my first lover, a young Chinese chef whose cock seemed enormous to me. When fully erect, his was an ear of corn, a long English cucumber, a banana, a carrot on steroids. So much for prejudice. I couldn't imagine that thing in me.

"Are you?" he asked. "I mean, haven't you ever..."

In the early sixties, we didn't talk about sex. If a woman was willing, it was assumed she had some experience. I was eighteen and worried I might die a virgin, which seems like a ridiculous fear now, but back then all my friends claimed to have lovers, and hinted that I couldn't be a woman until a man had made love to me. No, fingers didn't count (especially not your own), dildos didn't count, any orgasm without the aid of a penis didn't count. And other women? Oh, no, you wouldn't want to be one of those eternally virginal lesbians. Only a man could relieve you of your virginity.

My lover, whose name was Dave, was gentle, kind and creative, as American as his cock.

"Let me show you what I like to eat," he said as he lowered his lips to my cunt and began to nibble and lick, his tongue speaking a language I'd never known. He lifted his head to tell me my sauce was perfectly seasoned, then bent back down to suck and lap, murmuring, "Num, ummm, nummm, nam, nam, ummm."

I'd come many times before, from my own fingers, or a boyfriend's, and the first time while playing nurse with a girlfriend, but this was different. Was it because his penis, still hard, was brushing my leg as he lapped what he called my delicious juice? I felt like all of me had liquefied.

After I came, he knew not to stop his tongue until my throbs diminished.

"I need to make something for you," he said. "I'll be right back."

I watched him go into his kitchen, and imagined possible Chinese delights he might create for us. Crab puffs? Pot stickers? Almond cookies? Certainly not fortune cookies, which he'd dismissed as cardboard novelties for tourists. But it was too soon for the postcoital snack I was in the mood for. He hadn't come yet.

He came back waving a carefully peeled, long, narrow carrot, which he held against his own erect root.

"For you," he said, as if he were presenting me with a wonderful new dish he'd created.

"Is that a carrot?" I tried not to sound disappointed.

"I have a new way to prepare it," he answered, kneeling beside me on his bed.

He rubbed that carrot across my cunt, coating it with my sauce, then slowly inserted the narrow end, moving it carefully around, stretching me so gently I felt only pleasure. He pulled it out, then inserted the wide end deeper inside, rotating it carefully in circles.

I giggled at the thought that I was losing my virginity to a vegetable, but it was wielded by a man, and a cook at that, so it must count. My pleasure grew like a pot beginning to boil. I came again, my cunt walls clutching that carrot.

"Perfect, this will be perfect," he said, taking the carrot out, then sniffing it like a connoisseur.

At last it was time for dessert, that giant sweetmeat I felt so ready for. He raised himself above me, rubbing his cock across my slit as he'd done with the carrot, then inserted that final treat, which didn't feel a bit too large. My expanded cookie jar easily accepted the whole thing. I felt the pulse as he came, felt his liquid wash into me, but, worn out by that carrot, I didn't come again.

"There's more," he said after he'd caught his breath. "Stay still, don't move."

He went back to the kitchen and returned with a handful of grapes.

"Spread your legs," he said as he lowered his nose to sniff my cunt. "Perfect," he added as he inserted the grapes one by one until I was full.

"Wait a minute, if you can," he said, but I felt myself begin to tingle from the pressure of all those grapes. "Hold on," he ordered, and I did as long as I could, but the throbbing took me over and my orgasm popped those grapes right out.

He picked one up and ate it. "Ah," he said. "A savory sauce is so good with fruit. Here, try one." He pressed a warm grape into my mouth.

I was reluctant, but as I bit down, the combination of sweet tart grape and salty liquid filled me with a pleasure that was both gastronomic and sexual.

"Your sauce is still in there, too," he explained. "That adds an extra sweetness."

Then he took the discarded carrot back to the kitchen, where I heard him chop it, then open and close the oven door. He was back in five minutes with broiled carrot slices on a plate, perfectly seasoned with my own sweet sauce. We ate them with our fingers, along with the grapes.

Oh, we had many more cooking sessions, experimenting with different fruits and vegetables, and even sausages and strips of chicken and steak, which had to be precooked, though we always provided the seasoning.

When he went to France to study—French cooking was actually his specialty, not Chinese—time erased him from my life, but I'll always be grateful for what he taught me about fruits and vegetables.

Out of the bath I am warm and pulsing, perfectly ready, imagining my clean vegetables. I dry off, pull on a silk robe patterned in leafy greens, then drain my produce, soothe them with a coating of olive oil and carry them to my couch in a wooden bowl. Now to begin, but where? I lie back, trickle more oil onto my fingertips and massage my nether petals, paying particular attention to my stamen, which stands at attention. The pear is a good first choice, I think, the smooth stem end fitting neatly into the outer rim of my cunt as my well-oiled fingers circle my own stem. I am a fruit, a tree; my sap starts flowing.

I set the pear back in the bowl and take out the cucumber, still warm from its bath and much thicker than the pear, so I introduce it slowly, gradually working it deeper until it fills me. Carefully I twist it, turn it, press it to the top of my interior garden, mushroom sweet and sweating now. Outside my window, I see bare tree limbs sway in the wind, but inside I'm warm enough to let my robe slither off as I tighten my muscles around my firm, warm vegetable lover, strong yet silent, undemanding, loyal. I imagine I'll slice him up and eat him when he's been properly processed, which seems to be a fitting end.

For now I hold him in, tensing and relaxing, then gently pushing. My stamen throbs, sooner than I'd like because I want time to stop, I want to hold my breath to make myself eternal. As I relax and exhale, the slippery cucumber eases out, an untroubled birth, to be returned to the wooden bowl.

I want more. Vegetables aren't my only toys; my coffee table has a drawer of battery toys, and my bedside table contains the electric things. It's too much trouble to get off my couch of plea-sure, so I reach down and pull out my Jade Rabbit, with ears to tickle my clit and a shaft to go inside my pleasure garden, but the shaft is insufficient, too small, the vibrations lost in my folds. It's better to hold the rabbit's ears against my clit, with the shaft for additional vibration where it's most needed. Grow, bean! But then, fritz, fritz, there goes the rabbit, perhaps in need of new batteries.

I shake the rabbit, and he's alive again, for a while. Perhaps he needs a carrot; bunnies love carrots, and there's a lovely big one in my salad bowl. It's not too wide and goes in just deep enough. Perfection. I give Jade Rabbit another shake until he quivers against my hard berry, ripening by the minute as I wag the carrot back and forth inside me until I gush salty and sweet, pushing out the poor carrot, which has become a bit wet and limp from my hot juice.

My garden needs dessert; it needs cherries. One, two, three fit neatly inside, and then a fourth, making a real cherry pie. My quim, my valley, squeezes and relaxes, holding those cherries, letting the last quivers soften them until they're just right, warm and salty sweet. I pull them out one by one and suck them, spitting the pits into the ashtray on my coffee table, until there's nothing left.

I'm hungry after I've languished a bit, so I wrap myself in my robe, pick up my wooden bowl and carry it to the kitchen to make myself a large salad. I wash the lettuce and spinach, tear the leaves, then peel and slice half the cucumber, not too hard, not too soft, but just right. The carrot is almost parboiled because my body was much more steamy when I got to it, so I cut it into thin disks instead of grating it. I slice a tomato, and add some chopped pear because I love mixing fruits and vegetables. And for protein, some Gorgonzola cheese, which blends so well with the pear, the cucumber, the half-cooked carrot. I need no dressing, just a bit more olive oil mixed with the remnants of the salty, creamy juice that still oozes from the carrot and the pear. I devour the whole thing. Nothing has ever tasted so good.

THE CURE
FOR THE
COMMON LAY

Valerie Alexander

Hot, vivid pink and glowing. That's my first impression of the Simulsphere. Upon plugging in, the tunnel I find myself in is quite overtly vaginal, and I can't help rolling my eyes at the heavy-handed symbolism here. So much for innovative virtual reality designers. Give someone the opportunity to create a virtual world and the most imaginative thing he can come up with is a giant enveloping pussy. That is some serious creative failure right there.

Then I remember that the doctors can see my thoughts, thanks to the machine that's making this experience possible. This isn't old-school virtual reality, when a simple visual and auditory environment was exciting, and you had to wear the awkward headsets and datagloves and boots just to plug in. (Not to mention that once you were in, latency could freeze or snag the environment at any time.) Omni Labs has taken virtual to the next level, with amplified processing power, image resolution, communication bandwidth and geospatial sensors—and now their new machines that use over a hundred magnetic field detectors to record and scan my brain waves.

The result: a cocreated, collaborative environment. The Simulsphere has defined parameters, but those of us plugging in have the power to create furniture, animals, our own clothes, just by thinking about it, until we consciously dismiss them. In the case of tonight, we'll be creating a virtual orgy. Even though *orgy* is such a bestial-sounding word for such sophisticated technology.

Either way—the doctors back in the real world can see my thoughts, or guess at them at least, by monitoring my neurons through the machine. So I try to stop thinking about the ridiculousness of this soft, pink tunnel and instead think about my date tonight. Guaranteed to be gorgeous, anonymous and temporary: the perfect man.

I stop at the end of the tunnel, which opens into an enormous space that's like a black aquarium of neon fish. A mass of beautiful people are before me. Most everyone here has a simself that is some type of sexual stereotype: centerfolds spread their legs for cavemen, violet-haired nymphs lick Amazonian warriors like kittens, pretty boys in corsets and fishnets strip down for uniformed firemen and next to me, a mermaid is sucking off a muscular and handsome pharaoh in a white kilt and Egyptian headdress. It's like a kinky Halloween party where everyone has magic powers.

So this is what the gamut of human fantasies looks like, projected straight from the average tech worker's brain. Because I know these have to be industry people in real life, possibly even other Omni Labs employees—most outsiders aren't that comfortable with the new technological hedonism yet. Some of my coworkers might even be here. That's a decidedly unsexy thought, but I can't help mentally going through my team, thinking who'd be mostly likely to get their freak on virtually by rolling around in cake and having it licked off their nipples.

The video room from work begins to form in front of me. Shit.

Focus, Stacia, say the doctors in their unnerving god-like tech omniscience. It sounds like an echo inside my head. *Stop thinking about work or that's what you'll see.*

"Sorry."

Back to thinking about him. My date. The unknown man who was assigned as my partner in this trial. His simself will have black hair, brown eyes and be dressed as a solider; that's all I know. They wouldn't tell me if this is his first time in the Simulsphere too. It's actually my second, if you count last time, when I went into a private simulation designed to look like a beach. I'd plugged into plenty of regular virtual environments by then, of course, but this was my first time in a collaborative environment and it was intended to teach me the basics of directing the experience. It was also, I suspected, intended to help me get comfortable masturbating in front of the doctors, though they didn't say that.

I hadn't lasted long. The sand had that hot, baked feel under my feet and a breeze ruffled my hair—but then I realized I couldn't smell the ocean. I tried playing with my pussy but I got so freaked out over how it *wasn't real* that I unplugged. Just jolted right out.

That's an option tonight. If it turns out I don't really want to fuck a stranger as badly as I think, if it turns out I'd rather have it in real life—real human hands on my tits and a cock thrusting up my ass, the risk of rejection and the awkward conversation and the wet sheets and used condoms on the carpet—I can always unplug. If I can't actually handle getting naked in a crowd, even though my simself, a vampy temptress in black leather, looks nothing like me, I can unplug for that reason too.

A bare-chested man walks up to me and smiles. "Are you male or female? In real life."

"What does it matter?"

"I guess it doesn't. Can I see your tits?"

My dress suddenly has a zipper down the front, so I unzip and take out my bare breasts for him—luscious, perfect, with the pinkest nipples. And suddenly there's an old-fashioned chaise by my side, so I lie down and pull up my skirt to show him everything. He sits down between my legs and begins playing with my cunt. To my surprise, my clit and my labia—every millimeter of exposed skin—feel extra-sensitive and swollen. I spread my legs wider.

Stacia. Your agreement was to meet your date.

Right. Somewhere there's a hot young solider wandering around, looking for the black-leathered temptress of his dreams. "Okay, okay. Next time, I don't want a date." I'd only signed up for one because I'd been afraid of not finding anyone here to have sex with me—a ridiculous concern, I see now. I shrug apologetically to the man and plunge back into the crowd.

This is a shared simulation. All of the guests around me are real people plugging in just like me. Virtual trials like this are somewhat exclusive; you have to know the right people to get invited to participate, after the bad press last year's mind scanners got. Omni Labs developed the technology to record thoughts and memories from the cerebral cortex and a major controversy blew up over privacy, legal concerns and "the valid fears that technology may be outpacing us." Ever since, Omni's been covering their asses with a flurry of bland PR campaigns, like news segments on the virtual red velvet cake that tasted better than anything in real life, and virtual shoe shopping and decorating your virtual summer house.

But those of us here tonight don't care about that. We're all here to fuck in a way we never could in real life, come dripping down our faces, cock after cock, impossibly hot, wet, slapping sex. Softer, hotter, tighter than velvet, whatever we dream of, euphoric rushes that feel like narcotic stars shooting through our brains. Acting out the very dirtiest taboos, the ones that flood our faces with shame. Fucking past all barriers, searing and intense. *I want you, and you, and you and you, and I want that, and that, I want it all, now,* and you can have it, without consequence.

Or so I've heard.

I think about how beautiful I am tonight. Feline and feminine with a slinky grace. Not at all like my real self, an aging rebel turned programmer with a shock of black hair shaved on one side, average face, nice tits, and intense arm scars from a botched wireless wrist implant. (It was just before they developed corneal implants wired for the Internet—I've always been an early adopter.) But then my dress starts to waver; I've focused too much on my real looks. So I think hard about my black latex dress, the femme fatale I'm here to be, but then I picture a dominatrix in black rubber and my outfit continues to shift.

Stacia, you have to appear as agreed or he won't recognize you.

"Right." Maybe this is too much work; maybe it's easier just to get laid the old-fashioned way. But then I think of the ambivalent flirting, the fussing with condoms and lube, the hookups that always seem to miss the mark. No. This is better.

I see women gathered around what looks like an electric garden. They lift their skirts as some kind of hot golden-apricot flower attaches itself between their legs. The women drop their heads and howl in ecstasy as the flower-mouths service them.

One half faints onto the floor but urges "Try it," before her friends drag her away.

I lift up my dress again. It's not really a flower, it's some kind of organic sex toy that slides over my pussy. I'm so sensitive that its mere touch is jolting. No different from using a vibrator, I tell myself, but then the flower turns warm and kind of buzzy and I gasp as an intensely erotic sensation sweeps up my skin, filling my breasts, electrifying my labia. It's not like being licked or fucked or buzzed, it's something different entirely. "Oh god," I blurt out and the girl next to me meets my eyes and shakes her head right before she swoons into a faint.

"There you are."

It's my date. Dressed in a vaguely military uniform, twenty-five or so, black-haired and pretty. I open my mouth to say hello but my blood is singing with bliss and I'm about to swoon myself when he catches me around the waist. He peels my dress down and plays with my tits as I erupt in a thunderbolt of an orgasm.

"Oh god." I sag against him, wave after wave of thunder rolling through me. The flower-toy finally retreats. But the young soldier holding me feels so good that I don't want him to let go of me.

I straighten up in my black dress, leaving my breasts exposed. Now that we're together, it doesn't matter if my appearance morphs a bit, but suddenly I feel quite settled. I'm doing it. I'm mastering the "stay," as the doctors put it.

I turn and look at him. Deep tan, cocky grin, almond-shaped dark eyes. The stiff cock protruding from his uniform pants looks huge.

"I'm Jack," he says. "And you're hot."

"Let's skip the small talk." I take his hand and we set off to explore.

This is a place where time is meaningless and desire is accelerated. Where strangers reach for each other in the electric-lit dark and refusals and acceptances are equally serene. We parade through the garden of sex dreams that is the Simulsphere. A thousand personal aphrodisiacs linger in the air, smells of cigarette smoke and raspberry lip gloss and gin-and-tonics. Americana scenes of a girl in a white bikini and red nail polish watching a very handsome boy take off his baseball uniform. A seraglio of naked men on silk couches. People fucking in midair like naked acrobats. Images flicker in suspension: real scenes from porn movies and regular blockbuster movies where the characters strip down and turn to each other. There are some virtual pros here tonight who know exactly how to manifest and hold their desired scenes. And flickering in and out, half-consciously, a phantasmagoria of blurred memories and associations running through the minds of the bodies twisting and fucking around us.

Jack and I pass a brick alley where a woman in an eighteenth-century petticoat is being ravished by pirates. A redhead in a purple dress walking five leashed men, who crawl on all fours beside her. A gang bang in a bar. It's never going to end.

You're becoming overwhelmed. If you'd like to move from spectator to participant, we suggest finding one area of interest and focusing on it, says the overhead, but I ignore the doctors because Jack and I have already spotted something: a vibrant turquoise glow. It's a pool. But from the people inside it, we know it's not water so much as an aquatic substance moving as waves of light.

I wade into it in my dress. Despite being tight black leather, the dress now floats up around my waist like crinoline, showing off my legs, my pussy, all of which are perfect, and I begin to understand the possibilities. Forget physics and physical limitations, we're all here to transcend. This is a world that collaborates.

I turn to Jack, only to find him dressed now in a white T-shirt and jeans. Just a normal guy, but a very good-looking one as he pushes back his wet black hair with a smile. He has waded in too, and his nipples show through his wet white shirt. I take his pants down by running two fingers down his hips.

The pool is wired with extra conductivity, begins the over-head.

"Shut up. Don't talk to me again unless necessary."

I pull Jack deeper into the pool by his cock.

Oh god. It's like magic, like the best vibrator in the world is inside my skin and unleashing euphoria into my every cell. No sex is necessary, I think, but then Jack reaches for my breasts and my skin fills with fire for him.

We dive into the deep. There's no oxygen here to bring us up to the surface, so we entwine like long-lost lovers, arms and legs holding each other in this weightless aquatic dream. His mouth is hot on me in the cool water, his hands touching my clit with electric intensity. Kissing a stranger underwater is endlessly absorbing. I wrap my hands around his cock and he pulls back to give in to the sensation, his black hair waving toward me in the water. Eyes closed, he looks like an ocean god. I make my hands hotter, change the texture of my fingertips, and he opens his mouth and howls in a primitive sound that travels through the pool.

This isn't real, I think, but of course it is. My pounding heart is real. My stiff nipples, the ache in my pussy, the electric points of light in the water stimulating my skin, are real. Sensation and emotion are all that matters; I understand that now.

Fucking underwater is a kind of ballet, graceful and fluid between some of the couples around us and feverish and fast between others. We're all sexual magicians here. Jack sinks down between my legs and licks my clit, his tongue a sorcerer that knows just how to work all of me over, sliding inside my pussy, biting my lips, sucking the hard and buzzing seed of my clit. My body is a delirious symphony of sensation—and then I realize there's another man behind me, his tongue deep in my ass.

Don't come yet, don't come yet, I think, because I'm so afraid I'll unplug, but the two tongues inside me are too dreamy and I come with a hot ecstatic gush that explodes like bubbles in the pool. The environment goes hazy and I panic; but then both men hold me between them, and the hot solidity of their muscles anchors me back in the moment.

We stay underwater like that, a trio, for a few moments. Jack is looking at the other guy, who I haven't seen yet, so I slip to the side. The second man is the pharaoh who was getting his dick sucked earlier by the mermaid. They're looking at each other, not at me, maybe assessing who they are in this situation. I slide my arms around their shoulders and guide them into a long kiss that begins with hesitation, and then loosens into real passion. Orientation is just another dissolving boundary in this nebulous, melting world. Jack kisses me next, pressing all of his hard body up against mine. Now that my latex dress has disintegrated, I think myself into someone softer, more voluptuous, a woman wrapping around him like an enveloping pillow of skin.

Something hard presses my ass: the other man's dick. I push my hips back at him in invitation. He spreads my cheeks open and pushes his cock inside me, all the joy of anal with none of the caution because this pool is lube itself and everything here is smooth and painless. He holds me against him, fucking my ass hard now, making my breasts bounce up slowly in the water with every thrust.

Jack watches. He drifts down again to lick my clit, and the sensation of a soft tongue on my pussy and a hard dick in my ass make me want to drown in this white-hot glory. But if I'm going to come a third time, I know I'll lose the connection, and I need to make it count. I grip his hair, pull him back up and open my legs for him.

Jack fucks me like he's been waiting years for me. Hard, fast, relentless, just the way I like it. The other man matches his rhythm. Impossible, but we're doing it, cocks in my pussy and ass, thrusting with bionic strength and speed despite the waves rocking our bodies. There's no more question of veracity. The heat of their bodies is real, the grunts in my ear, the hairy legs abrading my thighs. The man behind me winds my hair around his fist, bites my neck hard. He comes as he does, a warm flood in my ass that washes through me like hot lava.

Jack's dark eyes change as he sees my own incipient orgasm burning in my face and he says with real urgency, "Not yet, not yet," words garbled underwater. Our connection is so intense that he knows I'm going to dissolve—and I do, a bomb of scarlet light and bliss that implodes in my pussy and then ricochets out in wave after wave through my entire body. The Simulsphere vanishes.

I unplug with that dizzying lurch. My brain feels like it was drop-kicked into my head, and a shudder of simulation sickness rolls through me. As the doctors liberate me from the machine, I think I might be caught between worlds. But no, I'm back. Firmly ensconced in this shivering body, as they help me stand. The room swims at me.

"Most people have trouble retaining the stay after they reach orgasm," says Dr. Oliver. "The fact that you stayed plugged in after the first and second climax is impressive."

I'm in a stupor. The naked woman in the mirror with the damp black hair and scarred arms doesn't seem that relevant anymore. My physical body feels more like a heavy limitation than anything. Just a happenstance swirl of genes, no more reflective of my true personality than my simself was.

"I'm sorry I messed up. I don't know why I kept picturing all those random things."

"You did better than many of the other trial subjects," says Dr. Helo. "It's natural for the untrained mind to leap around. Maintaining the stay in a collaborative environment takes practice."

"I would welcome the opportunity to practice, for as long as you're running the trial." All I can think of is how much money Omni Labs is going to make with this. Humanity will never be the same.

"You can participate on a weekly basis. Anything more frequent seems to be disorienting. That said..." They exchange a glance. "We have another experiment, another trial, if you're interested."

Dr. Oliver speaks to the conduit in his wrist and immediately a beautiful man walks into the room. Wavy blond hair, green eyes. His face is a combination of several beautiful actors.

I don't ask if he's real. That word no longer applies. The question is, is he organic, and the answer is no. That's clear from the flawless complexion, the vivid eyes and—I see the outline clearly in his Omni Lab pants—the size of his cock. Otherwise he looks quite biological. I try not to seem shocked, even though I had no idea Omni Labs had this level of biobots in development.

I do have one question, though, because suddenly I'm thinking about my hot tub at home. "Is he waterproof?"

"I am," the biobot says. "You can do anything with me you

can do with a human. Although you might find I do it better."
He smiles and it's actually a warm and sexy smile, not creepy
or artificial at all.

No different than a vibrator, I remind myself. I turn to the
doctors. "I'm interested."

CLAWS OUT

Rachel Kramer Bussel

C elia had to stifle a gasp of awe as she admired the shiny
metal claws glinting from her otherwise petite hand.
Normally, her manicure was short and trim—she did favor a
sexy, glossy-red color for her nails, but they were still the nails
of a size-four woman barely over five feet. Her size, though, had
nothing to do with her sexuality. Inside, she knew she was an
Amazon, a goddess, a woman capable of all sorts of wicked,
gloriously sadistic acts.

Over the last month, John had found out just how sadistic
she could be. She'd already tied him to the bedpost and tickled
him, holding a feather duster in her teeth. She'd had the most
fun with his cock. But of all the parts of his large, meaty body
she'd pinched and bitten and beaten, it was his back that was
most sensitive. She barely had to tap the suede flogger against
that sweet spot beneath his shoulder before his head was buried
deep in the pillow as he writhed.

Celia reluctantly took her new claws off, one by one, sliding the metal pieces from her fingertips and placing them back in the velvet pouch. They were gorgeous, a perfect symbol of her inner power manifested into something cool, sleek and dangerous— not that she'd ever truly hurt him. Her claws were about taking him right to the edge, where his skin prickled with fear and anticipation.

She kept them tucked away until the time was right. That night he was too jumpy, not in quite the right headspace. The next morning, though, she recognized the perfect opportunity. The sun glinted through her bedroom window onto her sumptuous black sheets, reflecting his rumpled, sleek back. John was a big man, but he'd been spared the voluminous hair that had plagued many of her other lovers. His was sparse, all the better for raking her claws down his back. She started by slipping a blindfold over his head, one so light he'd barely notice.

He only began to stir when she raised his hands above his head and twisted her panties into makeshift handcuffs around his wrists. "What's going on?"

"You'll find out soon enough, Sleeping Beauty." She ran the flat of her palm along his spine, down over the slope of one buttcheek, curving along his balls. She wanted to make sure he was, indeed, hard; otherwise the torment of keeping him on edge lost some of its appeal.

"That's what I like to feel first thing in the morning," she uttered as she reached beneath him and wrapped her hand around his stiff cock. John tried to buck into her touch, but she was too smart for that, and immediately dropped it.

"That's not what your dick is for," she snapped. His moan let her know he didn't mind one bit; being used as little more than a phallic prop turned him on like nothing else. Okay, maybe not quite as much as her taking him to the edge of pain and keeping him dangling on the precipice. Celia grabbed the pouch before straddling his waist, making sure her wetness met his warm skin. If she wanted to, she could simply hump him until she came, maybe use a vibrator to heighten her pleasure. But she'd have no problem getting off later; this was about a more lasting kind of pleasure, the kind she got from making sure he knew he belonged to her, through and through.

Before she broke open the pouch, Celia decided to play good domme for a little while longer. She leaned over to the bedside drawer, letting her nipples brush against his back as she reached for the massage oil. "Just relax." Those two little words could have multiple meanings—their simple, surface meaning, or their more twisted, sadistic opposite. She wasn't above telling him to relax right before she pushed the lever on his nipple clamps higher, tightening them on his nubs, or before she brought a vibrator up to his balls. It was up to him to read her well enough to hear beyond the dictionary definition, to learn her body language even when he couldn't see her. Only when he'd mastered that skill would she truly know he had long-term potential.

Celia warmed the oil between her hands, pausing to rub a little on her breasts, once again leaning down, this time to smear the warm liquid directly onto him. She added more, doing a sexy slip and slide before capping the bottle. Then she put her training as a masseuse to work. She'd done a stint as a massage girl, giving hand jobs but also true back massages; she'd been so good that the latter were what netted her the biggest tips.

Soon he was practically purring, putty in her hands—just where she wanted him. After digging her elbows into a few strategic spots, Celia stopped.

"Stay right there; I'll know if you move." She got up to wash her hands, and when she returned, she made sure to jingle the claws; the soft tinkling sound of metal on metal made him groan.

"I have a surprise for you, because I take good care of what's mine, don't I?" When all Celia got was a moan, she pinched the tender skin at the back of his neck. "Words, darling, use your words."

"Yes, you do. You always know what I like."

"That's more like it. Now relax; this will only work if you don't tense up."

Then she put the claws back on, transforming herself into what she considered her own version of Catwoman. She didn't need to dress up; the claws were all the costume she desired. With them on, she was a fierce woman with a weapon, one she chose to use for their mutual pleasure.

She waited until the only sound she could hear was John's heavy breathing. She shifted so the full weight of the warmth between her legs pressed down against him, then, steadying herself with her left hand on his upper back, she traced the tips of the claws from the nape of his neck on down. With barely any pressure, they still had a profound effect, if his breathing was any indication. "Well? What do you have to say for yourself?" she asked, before sinking them just a little more firmly into his soft, pliant skin.

"Oh my god," he sobbed, his body shaking as she made identical pink lines down his back. Celia had expected, to some degree, how turned on he would get, but the claws seemed to be working just as much magic on her. With each stripe she left on him, a corresponding jolt of excitement crept from his body back into hers.

She thought about writing her name on his back, but realized she didn't need to; her power and possession were there, on every inch of his skin, whether she was touching him or not. She shifted so she was kneeling against John, facing the expanse of his beautiful body, then moved her non-clawed hand so her fingers were curled around his balls. Lifting them, she stretched her thumb upward so it grazed his asshole. Then she raked her metallic claws down his back, harder than she had before. She didn't draw blood, but the lines were more vivid. The room crackled with energy.

"Are you ready to see what I've been using on you?"

This time she let him get away with a nonverbal response. When she rolled him over, John's cock greeted her. She'd been planning to keep teasing him—and herself—but the sight was too hard, as it were, to resist. She turned to make sure the panties were still snug around his wrists, her nipples dangling against his face in the process. When he strained to suck one nipple, she pulled back. "Not unless I say you can." Keeping her breasts just out of reach, she turned her hand so the flat of the claws could brush his cheek, smiling at the shiver that raced through him. "These you can kiss," she commanded, sitting up and bringing that same safe back edge of each claw to his lips.

Then, the claws having served their purpose, she slipped them off before slipping him inside her. She faced him, riding his cock while she used her natural nails to give his chest a similar treatment. This time, she could tell exactly what each scratch, each pull of the few hairs on his chest, did to him.

He knew he wasn't allowed to come until she did, but she liked trying to get him to anyway—all the better to punish him afterward. So when Celia said, "Next time, I'm going to tie you spread-eagle and use two sets of claws on your inner thighs," she was delighted to feel him explode inside her. Maybe "next time" would happen, well, as soon as she came. Good thing she'd bought an extra set.

SEX KITTEN

Errica Liekos

Sometimes he called her "kitten," other times "pet." She usually called him "Sir." She knew some couples did the Daddy/princess thing, but that never felt right to her. She liked being smaller than him, but she wasn't a little girl—she was a little animal. Rebellious yet affectionate, periodically demanding attention but otherwise low maintenance. "Kitten" suited her.

So from the moment she saw the display of tails at the Kinky Tea and Tag Sale, Allegra knew she had to have one.

"Aren't they fabulous?"

Allegra turned to see a smiling woman who appeared to be in her late forties or early fifties.

"I just got a new shipment," the woman continued. "We have some lovely arctic marble now; we've been out of it for a while."

Allegra stared at the tails, each clipped with a metal ring onto a horizontally strung wire, hanging like garments on a rack. There were maybe three dozen altogether, varying in shades of red, brown, black, white and silver.

"They're real?" she murmured.

"Fox and coyote. We have faux as well, if you prefer, but..."
The saleswoman's detailed explanations regarding the ethical
procurement of fur remnants faded into the background. Allegra
ran her fingertips across the silky collection. They swayed.

"How much?" she interrupted.

At home, Allegra gazed with reverence at her new purchase.
The tail itself was sixteen inches long, brown struck through
with black accents and a white tip. It *swished*. There had been
thicker and fluffier tails, longer ones, and ones with more
dramatic coloring, but this one moved exactly the way she
thought a tail should move: languorous, flirtatious, playful. The
small clasp that had once held the tail on a display wire was
now clipped into the loop set in the base of the tail's accompa-
nying glass plug. It was beautiful enough to leave out, Allegra
thought...if it could ever be appropriate to have a fox-tail butt
plug as home decor.

She checked the time—James was supposed to get out of his
last meeting of the day in only twenty minutes. She emailed to
tell him she had a surprise for him when he got home, then spent
the next hour furiously working her way through her closet and
dresser for the perfect accompaniments to her tail. Push-up bra,
no panties. High heels. Her basic black leather collar. (Why,
she wondered, had she never before thought of getting a bell to
hang from the front? So obvious.) Choosing a dress took longer,
as she insisted on precisely the right hem length to show off as
much tail as possible and have it appear as though it were an
utterly natural part of her body. By the time James's key clicked
into the lock of their front door, Allegra was quite sure that she
could hold her own against any of the sexy cat-girls she'd seen
in Japanese animation.

She walked toward her Sir, the sway of her hips deliberately calculated for maximum tail action. The tip of her tail wrapped around the outside of one leg with each step before flicking across to the other side. She twirled for her owner, did a full-on wag for his benefit, then faced forward to take in his reaction.

"I thought," James said slowly, putting down his brief-case, "that we agreed you wouldn't buy any more toys without discussing them with me first."

Allegra froze. She had, in fact, agreed to this rule after an unannounced shopping spree two months earlier. ("Pet, you cannot possibly need the same bullet vibrator in five different colors."

"They're not the same; look, each one has a different tip."

"Oh, please. You bought the whole set just because you thought they were pretty."

"...and that's bad?")

James hadn't actually said no to any of her proposed purchases since then, but of course the probability of him approving the purchase didn't change the penalty for failing to ask. The problem was that Allegra hadn't thought the tail *was* a toy.

She realized a case could be made that the tail was part of a costume and therefore fell into the unrestricted purchasing category of clothing. But the tail didn't seem like a costume to her any more than it felt like a toy. It didn't feel so inconsequential. It felt *real*. From the moment she realized that a fur tail plug was something she could have, not just a plush clip-on but something she could have inside her, a part of her body to swish and stroke and curl around her feet...it didn't feel optional.

She briefly considered apologizing, then decided against it. She wasn't a puppy, after all. She liked curling up at James's feet, but she was also the type to stretch a limb across his newspaper or keyboard, casually encroaching on whatever space was most central to his needs. She liked biting and scratching instead of talking to get his attention. *Some owners have submissives,* she thought, *and some have slaves. You, Sir, have yourself a cat. I want to rub up against you, pretending your focus isn't somewhere else. I want to demand you keep a hand free to stroke me, oblivious to your other obligations. I want to sleep in a sunbeam and stretch half the day, wander the house insolently, then settle in to find you've made me dinner. I have* opinions. *I'm the pet who owns you back.*

"My tail," she said pleasantly, "is not a toy."

James raised an eyebrow. "Really."

Allegra pivoted slightly to give him her profile once again. "Fur," she said. "Like hair. You don't make me ask permission before getting my hair cut, do you?"

"Not currently," James replied. "But now I'm thinking about it."

Allegra smiled, baring her teeth, and hissed at him. Then she wiggled her butt.

He sighed. "Oh, dear. What *are* we going to do with you?"

She batted her eyes, faux innocently.

"And after the day I've had..." James crooked his finger at Allegra, and she followed him to the couch, where he told her to kneel. He unbuttoned his suit jacket, sat, wrapped his hand carefully in her hair, then hauled her over his lap. With his other hand he flipped up her dress. The cool air swept over her ass, and she shivered. His free hand traced her jawline, then scratched her gently behind her right ear.

"What a dirty little kitten you are," James murmured. His right hand now ran up and down the length of her body. She arched gently under his touch. *Cats,* she thought, *always come when you call them...as long as they were planning to come to you anyway.*

"And what am I supposed to do about this?" James continued, stroking her tail. "Shall I spank you over it?" He grasped the tail in the middle and began running the free end of the fur up and down her legs. First the backside, then he nudged her legs apart and repeated the caress on her inner thighs. Allegra felt the fur brush against her cunt, and for a split second she worried what that would mean when it came time to clean up; she was sure she was sopping wet. Then she relaxed—it was a fox tail, after all. As though foxes in the wild never got wet or dirty. She spread her legs wider.

"Or shall I spank you under it?" James mused. Allegra purred, rolling her tongue against the front of her palate. James flipped her tail up, using one hand to trap it against the small of her back. His other hand grabbed her asscheeks, hard, before he started a series of playful smacks on the curve of her ass just barely above her thighs. Allegra purred harder.

"That's what I thought."

James spanked Allegra with thuddy, upsweeping strokes that turned her ass first pale, then hot pink. She mewed and kneaded the floor with hands curled into paws. And when he stroked her and petted her in between strikes, she purred and twisted to rub her head against his leg. He dipped his fingers inside her, testing how wet she was, and twirled the plug gently so that her tail spun in circles while she moaned. He alternated spanks with teasing, and didn't stop until she was squirming enough to have kicked off both of her heels. Then he ran his fingernails across her hot skin.

"Kneel up, kitten."

Allegra did as she was told, feeling the sheen of sweat on her skin. She briefly spread her legs, used her hands to flip her tail into a more attractive curl, then settled back into her place. The heat of her ass radiated against her bare feet.

"Now," James said, "I hate to be obvious about this, but would you like some cream?"

She would. He unzipped his pants and she pounced. She couldn't make the rolling *r* sound with her tongue while James's cock was in her mouth, but she quickly found another kind of purr building as she sucked, a deep rumble in her throat that was only silenced by swallowing down the sought-after prize. James kept his hand tangled in her hair until she climbed up off her knees and on top of him, butting him gently with her head and bullying him into lying down with her on the couch.

"I *did* have a rough day, you know," he said as she slid off his tie.

"Do you want to tell me about it?"

"Maybe later. Maybe a nap first." James kicked off his shoes and ran his hand down Allegra's spine. He grabbed her tail and wagged it for her. "Now, where exactly did you get this?"

Allegra smiled. "The Kinky Tea and Tag Sale I told you about. There was this magic wall of tails to choose from. They clip in." She raised her ass up, and James's fingers briefly touched the loop at the base of her plug, the small metal clasp that held the tail in place. He hummed his approval.

"Why didn't you get red to match your hair?"

She wiggled her butt. "This one was just so long and swishy..."

James used the tip of her tail to stroke the backs of her knees, then reached up to stroke her face. "Red," he repeated. "To match your hair."

"Yes, Sir."

"And black," he said, pulling her closer so her head rested in the hollow of his shoulder. "To match that other minidress I like so much."

"And white so I can be an arctic fox snow queen?"

"You are a kitten of many moods," James said. Allegra could feel his breath deepening against her hair. "One must be able to express oneself."

"You're a good owner," she said.

"And you're a bad kitty," he replied. He reached out a hand to set a half-hour alarm on his phone, then wrapped his arm around her. "Sleep now. Dry clean suit tomorrow."

"Yes, Sir," she said again. She cuddled closer. Eventually, she drifted off as well, finding peace both in the rumble in James's chest, and the soft heat of fur still pressed to the back of her legs.

STANDARD OF CARE

Sybil Rush

Read it." Dr. Bloom tossed the patient's chart to Oliver.

Oliver caught the folder and managed to keep the papers it held from falling out. He fumbled it open and read aloud. "Patient is a thirty-six-year-old woman. Chief complaint: Anorgasmia. Health history unremarkable. Patient remains inorgasmic despite counseling on self-stimulation. No organic cause of sexual dysfunction is apparent."

"Look," Dr. Bloom said, "as you all know, the medical board has recently rescinded the prohibition against sexual contact with patients in specific circumstances such as this one. However, the hands-on therapy you'll be learning to perform today is cutting edge. These cases are going to be scrutinized carefully, so proceed with the utmost discretion. At a minimum, always be accompanied by a female staff person." He indicated the nurse at his side, a tall woman whose scrubs were covered with cartoons of chimpanzees eating bananas. She nodded. "And be careful to document *everything*." He lifted the surgical mask from around his neck and tied it so it covered the lower half of his face. He pulled gloves out of his pocket and snapped them over his hands, then went into the patient's room, followed by the nurse.

All the residents tied their masks over their faces, including Oliver, although he wondered why it was necessary. He gloved up and followed Dr. Bloom into the examining room.

Inside, a woman lay with her feet in stirrups, wearing a pale-green hospital gown. As the residents encircled her, she looked steadily at the ceiling. Her breasts rose and fell. Oliver focused on her face, not on the little tents her nipples made in the thin cotton covering them. He checked the chart again to make sure of her name. "Vanessa?"

She turned big eyes toward him and nodded.

He glanced at the chart again, and then back at her face. "It says here that you're seeking treatment because you've never been able to have an orgasm. Is that right?"

"Yes. At least I don't think I have. They said you have an experimental treatment that might help me." Her voice was low, sexy. Almost like a smoker's rasp, but she didn't smell like smoke, didn't have the telltale lines around her lips.

"It's not exactly experimental," he said. "I'm going to use a vibrator, along with some verbal instructions. It's now the standard of care in cases like yours."

She looked disappointed. "It won't work. I already tried a vibrator. It didn't do a thing for me."

Oliver cleared his throat. "I understand. That's what it says in your chart. But some women need the doctor's touch, at first. If I can bring you to orgasm here, today, then I should be able to teach you to do it on your own, or with a partner. I'm going to remove your gown now, if that's okay." He untied the strings from around her neck and she raised her arms so he could lift the gown from her body. Her nipples were small, pink, puckered. Goose bumps stood up on her thighs, and she was shivering.

Oliver wondered whether she was cold or nervous. He moved so that he was standing between her legs. The nurse plugged in the vibrator and handed it to him. He was acutely aware of the gaze of the other residents. They all stood perfectly still, watching him from above their masks. He raised the vibrator, and located the ON/OFF switch and speed control. He'd observed a doctor perform this therapy before, but this was his first time. He tried to keep his hand steady.

Vanessa's eyes got even bigger and she tried to scoot back from the edge of the table. "You're not going to stick that in me? It's too big!"

"No, no, this is a wand-type vibrator. I'll just be using it on the outside of your body." *How did she not know that?* he thought. *Surely her therapist had explained how to use a vibrator? It doesn't matter now. Concentrate.* Oliver brushed the curls back from her pubic mound so he could more easily see her vulva. Her clitoris was small, deeply hooded, almost hidden in her pink lips. He turned the vibrator on LOW and pressed it gently against her.

"Oh," she said. Her face took on a look of wary concentration.

Dr. Bloom pushed his way between the two men to Oliver's right. He addressed the residents as if Vanessa wasn't in the room. "You don't want to rush things at this point. Watch the patient. Wait until she habituates to the sensation. You want her to relax enough to begin to get bored." Sure enough, as if on cue, Vanessa's legs released open and she looked around the room.

Dr. Bloom nodded to Oliver. "Now's the time to increase the intensity."

Oliver switched the vibrator to high and pressed it firmly against Vanessa's vulva. She began to pant. She wrapped her arms across her chest, squishing her breasts. "I can't stay relaxed," she said.

Ignoring her statement, Dr. Bloom addressed the residents. "Part of the problem is that these women have often been told, 'Just relax, and it'll happen.' But orgasm isn't brought on by relaxation. It requires rhythmic muscular tension." He raised his voice to address Vanessa. "You just hang in there, young lady. Won't be long now."

A bead of sweat dripped from Oliver's forehead onto his mask and an erection was growing inside his scrubs. He was glad that they were all wearing plastic aprons so no one could see the lump in his crotch. He wanted to touch Vanessa's nipples, which were now bulging between her fingers as she clutched at her breasts. He wanted to rub himself against her bare buttocks, where they protruded off the end of the table. He peeked furtively at the other residents, wondering if their dicks were hard, too. Then he pushed the thought out of his mind and pressed the vibrator more firmly against Vanessa's clitoris.

"The patient is showing all the signs of impending orgasm," Dr. Bloom said. "Her respiratory rate has increased. She's exhibiting the characteristic involuntary large-muscle contractions. Note the sex flush on her upper chest, forehead and cheeks. The breasts have increased in size and the nipples are erect. The vaginal lips have reddened and become enlarged as well, due to vasodilation. You can observe them moistening."

Vanessa's eyes were closed and her breath made small rhythmic sounds. "Oh, oh, oh." She squirmed. *Is she trying to get away from the sensation? Or trying to press herself closer to it?* Oliver wasn't sure. Suddenly her eyes flew open and looked straight into his. "Oh fuck!" she screamed. "I'm coming. I'm coming!" She grabbed his wrist and pulled his hand, with the vibrator, hard against her vulva. Her back arched and her head rolled from side to side.

Just as suddenly, she pulled his hand away from her body and sat straight up on the hospital bed. She threw both arms around Oliver and hugged him, laughing and pressing her face into his chest. "It worked! I can't believe it. Doctor, I could kiss you!" Her feet were still splayed in the stirrups, high up next to her ears. As she pressed her breasts against him, Oliver looked around, surprised and embarrassed. He patted her nude back awkwardly. The vibrator still buzzed away in his other hand.

After a few moments, Vanessa lay back with both hands behind her head and sighed. "That was amazing." Oliver switched the vibrator off and handed it back to the nurse.

"Well done," Dr. Bloom said. "Now, how many of you have erections?" The residents looked around sheepishly. One by one, they slowly raised their hands. Oliver raised his as well. "Exactly. So do I. Now, the new protocols state that it is acceptable to have intercourse with the patient, as long as the patient consents and the treatment is deemed therapeutically desirable." He raised his voice again. "Vanessa?"

"Yes, doctor?"

"Following the therapy you just received, we expect that you should be able to have orgasms on your own in the future, by using a vibrator. However, many women are not satisfied with this outcome. They don't consider the treatment a success unless they are able to orgasm with a partner. For most women, it's much easier to orgasm during intercourse if they have recently orgasmed from direct stimulation. Do you understand?"

"Yes, doctor."

"Then, with your consent, we will proceed to part two of the therapy."

"Yes, Dr. Bloom."

Dr. Bloom turned to Oliver. "You may proceed."

Oliver hadn't been expecting this. "What should I...I mean how should I..."

Dr. Bloom said impatiently, "Well, don't just stand there, young man! You're a doctor."

Oliver looked to Vanessa for guidance, but she was still lying on the narrow bed with her arms behind her head, waiting with an attitude of relaxed expectation. He untied his scrub pants, pulled out his erect penis and rolled a condom onto it. "Lube," he said. He held out his hand, and the nurse squirted a dollop onto his fingers. He massaged it onto the head of his cock, and then smeared the rest onto Vanessa's labia. He slipped gloved fingers inside her. She sighed and her eyelids half closed. Everything about her felt soft and open.

He spread her lips with his fingers and slid his cock into her cunt. It slipped in easily and her snug, warm walls surrounded him. He pushed all the way in, so his hip bones pressed against the firm muscles of her buttocks that bulged over the end of the table. He stood there for a moment, not moving, inserted all the way to the root of his cock. She was wiggling against him, trying to rock her hips up and down, but not really able to because of the table and the stirrups and her ass suspended out in the air. She looked so pretty, struggling like that, with that pleading look on her face. He started to stroke in and out of her. She moaned and closed her eyes.

"At this point," Dr. Bloom said, "you could apply the vibrator again." He paused. "On second thought, I don't believe you'll need it. Digital stimulation should suffice."

Oliver took Vanessa's hand and placed it on her cunt. He positioned her fingers on each side of her clitoris and used his thumb to set them moving rhythmically back and forth. A look of amazed understanding came over Vanessa's face and she began to rub herself vigorously. She made little yips and cries and the pink flush spread across her chest and cheeks again.

"A little nipple stimulation would not be out of order, doctors," Dr. Bloom said. The two residents nearest Vanessa's head jumped guiltily and each gingerly pinched a nipple. Oliver stroked his erection into her harder and faster. Vanessa screamed and her cunt gripped him. That was it. He was coming along with her, grasping on to her shapely thighs and inhaling her salty scent.

When the intensity of the pleasure receded, Oliver slowly pulled out. His fellow residents were softly clapping their gloved hands. A few of them whistled. Vanessa smiled shyly.

As he walked toward the sink, Dr. Bloom clapped Oliver on the shoulder. "Well done," Dr. Bloom said. "You'll make a fine erotologist."

BIKERY

Oliver Hollandaize

It was one of those rare warm evenings in San Francisco, the kind that comes after a hot fall day. All the outdoor tables at the café were taken, which was why Suzi and I were sitting inside, sweating along with our pints of cold beer. Outside, bikes were locked to every available vertical fixture, including the spindly saplings that lined the block. The slice of sky over Valencia Street was fading into a sultry darkness, and it seemed like everyone was up for a long night even though it was only Tuesday.

At least we had a table by the big open window so we could watch the crowd out on the sidewalk. I noticed a couple at the curb and gave Suzi a nudge. He was lanky and broad-shouldered, leaning against the crossbar of his bike with his back to us, a filigree of colorful ink decorating both his long arms. She was as tall as he was, with a serious face softened by a warm smile, arching brows, dark eyes and a strong jaw. I watched her face over his shoulder, her eyes moving down to his mouth, then away with a laugh, a flash of pink tongue wetting her lips. She held her bike between them, a barrier across her hips that she leaned into as they talked.

We watched him drop his hand to the seat of the girl's bike, then languidly trace the length of the crotch-polished leather with his index finger, from back to front then back again. I saw her try to suppress a squirm, taking in a quick breath, blushing and laughing.

"Smooth," Suzi said appreciatively, tucking a strand of unruly blonde hair back behind her ear as she leaned over her beer, her greased-stained hands cradling her small, round face. Suzi was an artist who'd gotten her start building kinetic sculptures for Burning Man and now had several gallery shows under her belt. She was also a mechanic at one of the trendiest bike shops in the city, five blocks up the street. "Bikes are sexy, no doubt about it."

"Yup, they are, but why is that?" I asked.

"I think it's all about the saddle really. For one thing, it shows off an ass like nothing else. Bike seats are pedestals for the ass. They make average asses into fucking works of art."

I nodded. "It can be hypnotic. I almost died that way once, following a girl through a red light."

"And another thing," she continued. "The bike saddle is one of the few things specifically designed to snuggle into the crotch like that. It's not a big leap of imagination to go from thinking about bikes to thinking about pussy, as demonstrated by our friend out there." She nodded toward the window.

"And when did you make that leap of imagination?" I asked.

"Oh, I don't know exactly, but I guess I've been into bikes ever since I was fourteen and inherited my older sister's with a seat that was a little to high for me. I came all over that thing—

rode it so much that summer, my cunt ached all time. I didn't adjust the seat though!"

"Came?" I asked. "I always thought that was bullshit that girls could have orgasms from riding bikes."

"Oh no, it's absolutely fucking true." She smirked into her glass and leaned back in her chair.

"All I ever got from my bike was bruised balls when I'd fall on the crossbar," I grumbled.

Small and looking younger than her midthirties, Suzi was one of those women who'd get carded until she went gray. She looked particularly cute when she talked about sex, a favorite topic of ours. Her peaches-and-cream complexion and compact, strong body gave her a girlish innocence, an impression that she delighted in subverting with her pornographic vocabulary.

"I can't believe you never told me about that before! It explains a lot—like your job." I gestured to her grease-stained hands. "Do you still come riding bikes?"

"Sometimes," she said flirtatiously. Then, after hesitating for a second, she leaned across the table with an impish look I'd learned to recognize as a sign that I might get lucky. "Let's go to my place. I want to show you something. You'll like it."

Suzi mostly dated girls but she'd occasionally requested my friendly cock when she'd had a craving; I'd happily come along for the ride. There was a hopeful stirring in my jeans as I imagined what she might be hungry for tonight. I knew that she knew exactly what I was thinking but she refused to tell me anything in spite of a long series of my best sexually exaggerated facial expressions: raising an eyebrow, lip-biting, winking, along with nudges and flirty kicks under the table.

"Okay, I'm ready to go." I drained my glass in a couple of large gulps. She giggled a little too loudly at my eagerness to leave. Was she nervous? That wasn't like her and made me even more excited, requiring a covert through-the-pocket adjustment as I got up from my chair.

Her place was three blocks away, an old carriage house hidden behind a larger building that might have once been a stately home. She let me in through the heavy wooden door and flicked on the light of her studio, a sprawling workshop with a kitchen set up in a far corner. Her bedroom was on the top floor, so I turned toward the stairs.

"Uh-uh. Over here, dummy!" Taking my hand, she led me across the shadowy space, around crates of salvaged parts glinting in the dim light, battered toolboxes and welding equipment. Sculptures in various states of completion rose from the scarred and blackened floorboards like machines from a postapocalyptic civilization. In the far corner a space had been cleared away and a semicircle of mismatched chairs had been drawn up around a stained canvas tarp covering a bike-like form.

"You expecting an audience?" I asked, gesturing to the chairs.

"Maybe. I'm thinking about it. But you're the first to see this. I finished it a couple days ago." Pulling off the tarp, she revealed what used to be a bicycle but was now something much, much more.

I took a few steps back. "Shit, that's amazing! It's beautiful, Suzi! What is it?"

The shiny, black tubes of the frame and the sweeping chrome of the handlebars gave the thing the appearance of a beach cruiser made for a vampire, but it was obvious that this bike wasn't meant for actually going anywhere. Instead of holding a wheel, the front fork swept down with a serpentine curl to the floor, supporting the frame. Delicate gold-and-white pinstriping flowed across the dark armature, and the words BOINK BIKES LTD. decorated the crossbar.

Like the front, arching struts supported the back of the bike frame, and a large, heavy-looking silver disk took the place of the rear wheel. "That's the flywheel," Suzie pointed out. "And see here? This is where the magic happens." She pointed to where a second chain ran from the flywheel up to a dense assembly of clockwork under the saddle.

The saddle itself was a sleek wedge of black leather with a horn that curved upward to cup the rider's crotch. "I think I get the idea, but that thing doesn't look very comfortable." I pointed to the bare metal rod poking up through a hole in the middle of the seat. Suzi pressed a short, thick red dildo down onto the rod. She reached down to give the leather-wrapped pedals a quick spin with her hand until the flywheel was turning, and then flicked a lever on the handlebars. The machinery below started a rhythmic whir as the dildo vibrated and writhed like a sea cucumber doing the hula. I blushed at the mental image of Suzi riding this thing.

"Take a seat," she said in a businesslike voice, nodding to a sagging velour armchair behind me.

"Okay!" I grinned nervously and flopped down into the dusty upholstery.

"I'm feeling shy now, but fuck it. I'm going to just pretend you're not here for a minute, okay?" She turned her back and unceremoniously pulled off her white cotton tank top, then undid her belt and peeled her jeans and panties down to the floor. My breath caught at the sight of her nude body, her skin a creamy white except for the freckly farmer's tan on her arms and neck. She kicked the tangled wad of her clothes aside and turned around.

"Okay. Now some lube just to get things started." She picked up a bottle from the floor, squeezed a generous dollop into her palm and stroked the dildo to a slippery shine. I stirred in my seat, my cock trying to poke up under the waistband of my pants in solidarity.

Suzi slipped her lubed hand between her legs, her fingers dipping in and then out again to give her clit a few light rubs. Wiping her hands on a rag, she threw a leg over the crossbar and stepped up onto the pedals. She reached back and held the dildo in position as she slowly lowered herself down into a riding position, the thick cock sliding into her. Taking a breath, she took hold of the handlebars, closed her eyes and began to pedal. When the silver flywheel was spinning with a heavy whir she thumbed the lever upward. The clockwork under the seat shuddered rhythmically, and Suzi with it. "Fuck yeah!" she groaned loudly and threw back her head, mouth open in a sigh of pleasure.

She turned toward me now, confident and flushed. "Now watch this," she said, and with the flick of a switch lights flickered on from somewhere on the frame, bathing her face and swaying breasts in a pulsing red glow. "Feel free to pay homage to my creation," she added with a melodramatic sweep of her arm, nodding in the general direction of my erection.

I pulled off my shirt, wriggled my jeans down around my ankles and gave my rigid cock a liberal squirt from her bottle of lube. It was time to take in a full account of this pedal-powered erotic tour de force. Suzi had found her cadence and looked utterly transported, eyes closed, her hair sticking to her face and shoulders as she pedaled and moaned and swore softly to herself. I stroked away to the rhythm of her machine, watching pleasure sweep across her face, my balls tight with anticipation.

She was caught by surprise as her first orgasm surged through her. Watching her suddenly writhe and curse with pleasure, I could feel the same stabbing urge to come lapping at the base of my spine. I quickly pulled my hand off my shaft and closed my eyes, warm precome spilling onto my belly.

When the fluttering deep in my crotch subsided I opened my eyes to find her watching me intently through heavy-lidded eyes, pedaling slowly. "Shit, that was close!" I groaned. "I want to wait and come with you." I trailed my fingers through the slippery drops on my belly and lifted them to my mouth. "Mmmm, look what you're making me do," I teased her.

"Fucking pervert," Suzi chuckled, and bit her lip in that utterly adorable way of hers, thumbing the lever on the handlebars again as she began to pedal in earnest. The red lights pulsed faster; her head dropped between her shoulders as she murmured obscenities in a tight, husky voice. I knew she was close so I stroked slowly, trying to pace myself, but I wasn't going to be able to take much more of this amazing erotic spectacle.

Thankfully I didn't have to wait long. Her knuckles were white on the handgrips now, her eyes shut tight and her lips pulled back over her teeth as she gasped for breath. Then her face softened in a spasm of slack-jawed pleasure and she yelled out and bucked on the seat as she came. I had a second to take it all in before a final tug on my slippery cock blinded me. An endorphin-soaked firebomb detonated in my head with a whoosh, and, as if from a great distance, I felt come splash on my chest as my body jackknifed and shuddered in a cataclysm.

When I opened my eyes I saw that Suzi had stopped pedaling and lay draped over the handlebars in a sweaty mess. The flywheel still whirred behind her but the clockwork was disengaged and still. She slowly stood up, letting the dildo flop out of her, wobbled over and collapsed into the chair next to me. "Holy fuckin' shit. It made it even better having an audience. I loved having you watch me!"

"Anytime," I mumbled. Then I asked, "Are you going to build something like that for guys?"

Suzi looked me over with sex-glazed eyes, from where my jeans were still gathered around my ankles up to the ribbons of come decorating my chest. "I think I already have," she said, smirking, then kissed me softly on the mouth and tossed me a greasy shop rag.

PENCIL DICK

Kathleen Delaney-Adams

She took my ass on a filthy bedspread at a motel on Cheshire Bridge, the kind of scumbag place that didn't offer its disreputable patrons soap or towels or even toilet paper, the kind of place that you could rent by the hour. I was facedown in my own ejaculation, tits smashed into the mattress, my legs spread open by her knees, my insides feeling torn open all along the length of my spine. In short, I was in high femme heaven.

I have the tightest little asshole in the world, I swear it. I have references that will attest to this fact. It could take a small construction company to drill and pound and crack it open. But she was game—if game meant long and mean and strong enough to pin me down and crack me open. She seemed to be enjoying herself back there, making wiseass comments in that Southern drawl I was half-wild for, hissing things like, "You are such a cock-teasing whore." There is not much a filthy girl like me would not give for moments like this, and if my asshole had to be sacrificed I'd be the first to offer it up like a lamb.

How I came to be in this whorish position has much to do with my big mouth and less to do with her being the finest butch this side of the Mississippi. I'll admit I was a bit full of bravado the night we met. Fresh from a promotion to Practice Manager at the clinic, I was raucously celebrating at Mary's Bar with a cluster of gay boys every bit as femme as I. I spotted her the instant she strutted in with a cool butch swagger that soaked my pussy. *You* know the kind of butch I'm talking about, a salt-and-pepper Daddy who makes you want to fall over onto your back and spread your legs before she even says hello. What was a femme to do but tease and flirt and eye that bulge in her jeans suggestively?

Okay, so I crossed a line when I began bragging about what a size queen I am. Indeed, my exact words may have been, "Being a filthy whore, I can take it up the ass." I did not feel compelled to tell her that the only thing I had ever actually had up my ass was an embarrassingly small, alarmingly blue cock my ex strapped on and tried to squeeze inside my hole while I clamped it tightly closed and sobbed into my pillow. At the time, I lovingly referred to this appendage as "pencil dick." At this very moment, with a gorgeous stud leaning against me and the slickness between my thighs making me disoriented, pencil dick had taken on enormous proportions in my mind. Surely it was ten inches thick and I had opened up easily for every inch? Unfortunately for me, that was the tale I chose to tell on this night. My misrepresentation of facts, fueled by lust, was to seal my fate: my challenge was met with a smirk and a dare, and a date was set. The game was on.

The morning of our first date, if you could actually call it a date, found me in an aisle of CVS, pondering the enemas. A girl had to be clean, did she not? The products displayed before me were ugly and medicinal. As skeptical as I was that I could take her butch cock in my ass, I felt desirous and full of feminine power, and did not want an ugly enema in my handbag ruining my mood. I perused the aisles until I found exactly what I wanted in the baby section. A pretty pink ear syringe should do the trick quite nicely. Perfect.

Preparation has always been my favorite foreplay, and I have been known to devote hours to the task. Pampering, self-indulgent bathing and primping, donning skimpy lingerie (or none) beneath skimpier dresses, the cherry on top a carefully selected and always killer pair of stilettos.

By the time I left the house I was already slick. My skin gleamed creamily, I was surrounded by an airy cloud of Vera Wang, and my holes—every last one of them—were clean and sparkling like polished gems. I was ready, and convinced my latest conquest could hear my heart hammering as I pulled into the parking lot.

Her choice of motels was fitting, with just the right amount of seediness to make me feel as if I were in the midst of a slightly dangerous, very sleazy act. She had texted that she was waiting for me in room 115. I paused outside the door to gain my composure. I was so hot for her, and my lust was dancing battles with my trepidation. I barely knew her, I didn't know how my ass would ever take that gargantuan rubber cock up inside it and what if she opened the door and I felt, well, *nothing*? Desire could come and go at a moment's whim, I knew that, and I feared mine for her was mostly in my head.

Taking a decisive breath, I lifted my hand to knock just as the door burst open. An enormous shit-eating grin on her face, she grabbed my arms and pulled me into the room, kicking the door shut behind her. The instant her mouth seized mine, all doubts slipped from my mind and I moaned, melting against her broad chest. My nails dug hungrily into her shoulders and our kiss became frenzied. I moved closer to grind myself into her crotch, and moaned again when I felt that bulge against my pussy. My legs opened of their own volition, and her grip on my arms tightened in response to my obvious need for her. I don't know what came over me, but I was rubbing my clit on her jeans and crying out and clutching at her. I was completely undone. I threw my head back and shouted out as I came with an abandonment that rendered me utterly useless.

She laughed in delight and lifted me into her arms. I wrapped my legs around her waist and threw my arms around her neck as she carried me to the bed. She laid me on it as if I were a priceless package and stared down at me like she couldn't wait to unwrap me.

Slowly, I lifted my little dress up over my hips, exposing myself to her. I spread my legs and offered myself up to her. She groaned and rubbed her cock through her jeans. One knee on the bed, she leaned over me and yanked my straps from my shoulders and down over my tits. My nipples hardened at the sudden cold air and her piercing stare on them.

She groaned low in her throat and swung one lean, hard leg over me, straddling me around my waist. I shivered deliciously at the sound of her zipper and the promise behind it. She untucked her cock and pulled it out, rubbing her hand up and down the shaft and smirking at me as I thrashed beneath her. How I needed that dick deep inside my pussy, and I mean *yesterday*.

She leaned forward and slapped my face with her cock, teasing me, provoking a response. How could I do anything but give it to her? My tongue chased it, aching to lap and lick. I cried out in frustration when she denied me.

"Not yet, whore. Maybe later."

Abruptly, she stood and crossed her arms, her cock dangling mockingly between her legs.

"Are you clean?" Her question felt more demand than inquiry.

I nodded.

"Answer me when I speak to you."

"Yes," I replied instantly.

"Are you sure? If you get my dick dirty I'll make you lick it off."

I hesitated, than asked permission to use the bathroom. She granted it with a curt nod, and I scrambled for my purse and the relative privacy of the toilet.

It was dank and filthy in the bathroom, but I relished the time alone to collect myself. I removed my newly purchased pink ear dropper and filled it with murky water from the sink. Crouching over the toilet, I filled my ass and released. Again. I cringed at the involuntary noises, hoping she couldn't hear me through the all too thin motel walls. Convinced there could not possibly be anything left inside me, I exited and stood before her once more, cheeks flushed with embarrassment.

Her eyes were kind, her mouth slightly upturned in what may have been a smile. My shoulders relaxed a bit and I moved toward her.

"I'm ready," I whispered, suddenly shy.

She inclined her head toward the bed, and I crawled onto it and lay on my back.

"Take off your clothes and roll over."

Slowly I removed my dress, the air-conditioned room chilling my skin. I hesitated, then left my heels on, feeling less vulnerable with the spiky points of my stilettos as a sort of femme crutch.

I rolled onto my stomach and waited.

She grabbed my hips and pulled me back toward her, lifting my ass high into the air.

"Perfect," she murmured, running her hands over my rounded

buttocks, squeezing until I yelped at the pinch of pain. She slapped my cheeks hard and fast, and heat spread through me.

I heard her rummaging around behind me and I held my breath, quivering with anticipation.

"Don't worry, doll baby, I'm opening you up first."

She worked my hole, rubbing thick lube around the opening. Her fingers plunged inside, first one, then two, and I moaned in protest when she withdrew them.

I felt cold hard rubber at the opening of my asshole. She began rubbing it slowly, achingly slowly, until I arched my back with desire, forcing the tip into my hole. Once inside she froze, leaving me wanting. I whimpered and squirmed on it, forcing it in a bit more, stopping at the quick stab of pain.

"That's it, whore," she whispered, "that's it."

She slid the rubber—what was it she was using?—in and out of my ass, increasing the depth with each push forward. I clutched the bedspread and thrashed and groaned, hungry for more despite the hurt and my anxiety. Harder and harder she moved it inside me, my cries escalating as I neared orgasm. She put her hand on the flat of my back, forcing me onto the mattress. One quick thrust and it was in as far as it could reach, filling me completely.

"Mmm, girl, you like my anchor, don't you?"

I nodded, then, remembering her instructions, I managed to croak, "Yes."

"I've got you right where I want you."

With excruciating slowness, she pulled the anchor inch by inch out of my ass, each movement causing spasms of need. When she pulled it completely out, leaving me open and wanting, I felt bereft.

Again, she slid a couple of fingers into my ass and rotated them.

"Good," she said. "Better."

I lay panting where she had left me, listening intently for sounds that would tell me what to expect next.

"On your hands and knees."

I rose into the air, limbs trembling with fear and lust and a massive hunger to be used by her. She grabbed my waist and pulled my ass back toward her. I heard the sound of a condom wrapper, her grunt of effort, my own heart pounding in my chest. Now. Now.

She leaned over and crooned in my ear, "Don't worry, baby. I'll go easy on you. At least at the beginning."

She chuckled and positioned herself behind me.

The first thrust was a sharp tear along my spine. I fell face forward onto the mattress, crying out. The pain was too much, too much, and I struggled beneath her as if to flee.

"Shh. Whore, didn't you say you could take this? Relax. Breathe. Breathe."

Breathing seemed to require every last vestige of concentration I had remaining, but I managed to gasp out a long exhale. I tried to relax my muscles, despite the searing pain. Patiently, she waited until I composed myself.

"There. The worst part is over. Now you had better keep me in."

She shifted her hips slightly and the pain intensified. Her movements were almost tender, and I felt the tension drain from my body as she took me. She pushed in all the way, allowing my sudden sharp cry of outrage, and she was still.

She paused, and began moving her cock in quick short jabs, gradually increasing the length and speed until my ass was being rapid-fire fucked. I may have been screaming, the pain unlike any I had ever experienced, but damn if I wasn't enjoying myself. It wasn't long before I was bucking wildly beneath her, shouting jubilantly. She grunted in time with her jackhammer thrusts, obviously getting off on taking me, and I was so hot for her it became unbearable. I shifted enough to slide my hand between my legs, fingering my pussy and rubbing my clit while she rammed me. Minutes, hours, I lost track of time. I lost track of everything but the glorious release as I came more explosively than at any time I could recall.

I lay splayed on the bed, unable to move, but still she pounded into me. I was certain I was torn open, so raw and sore I wasn't sure I could take another moment. I struggled to remember our agreed upon safeword, when she stopped moving. Her hands gripped my waist, her breath ragged in my ear, her cock plunged so deep I was sure she was in me up to my eyeballs. Her body jerked once, twice, then she came with a soft, low cry that soaked my cunt all over again. Spent, she fell on top of me and we were both still.

She felt wonderful on top of me, the full weight of her body curled around me. I sighed dreamily and nestled in, feeling satiated, if not downright smug. A small smile flitted about my mouth.

"Mmm." As if she shared my feelings, she murmured in contentment.

She shifted and touched my hair gently.

"Girl, I'm coming out now."

I nodded, bracing myself for what I was sure would be more agonizing pain, but she moved out of my ass smoothly and easily.

She pulled the condom off her dick, tossing it on the floor, than lay propped up on one elbow. She looked so damn sexy and just a bit vulnerable. It made me bold enough for the truth.

"Hey, I have a confession to make," I began.

"Shh." She put a finger on my lips and smiled. "I know all

about your confession, girl. Why do you think I went easy on you this time?"

I blushed and looked away. Then, realizing the implications of what she had just said, I raised my eyes to hers once more.

"*This time*? Does that mean, well, that there will be another time?"

She laughed wickedly, a sound that reverberated on my clit.

"Silly whore, I'm not done with you yet! In fact, I'm pretty sure I said I'd let you blow me if you took it like a good girl. That pretty mouth of yours should be used for more than getting yourself into trouble."

So excited at the prospect of that huge rubber dick in my mouth, I all but clapped my hands and did a cartwheel. She was still laughing when she reached over to grab another condom from the nightstand.

A TALE OF TWO TOYS

Chris Komodo

Can u feel it? he typed, from the back of the lecture hall.

Twelve rows below, a student with wavy blonde hair and stylish glasses squirmed in her seat. Long, low vibrations awakened her clit and sent waves of pleasure throughout the nerves in her body. Down in the front of the classroom, the professor drew another chemical bond on the whiteboard.

It felt wicked to get so aroused in the middle of lecture. The muffled buzzing inside her panties continued, and she prayed no one could hear.

She pulled her phone, in its pink Hello Kitty case, closer and tapped at the screen.

God, yes. fuck, i want you. now. She hit SEND.

Grinning with one side of his mouth, her boyfriend replied simply, *Not til tonite.*

At the same time, two hundred miles away, Matt and Kira were doing seventy-three down a snow-lined Montana highway toward the very same college town.

"Sex in public," she answered. "But you knew that one." Kira smiled, reaching over and placing her hand on her husband's thigh. He took his eyes off the road for a second and saw the mischievous glint in hers. The late-afternoon sun lit a halo around her long, black hair.

Matt thought how his wife looked as hot now at thirty-two as she had when he first met her ten years ago.

The couple were in the middle of a sorely needed getaway. They hadn't been anywhere alone together for long since their son was born six years ago, and this winter road trip through the Rockies would give them time to reconnect and—Matt hoped—put some fire back into their sex life.

"I think that's gonna stay a fantasy, though," Kira added. "I'd be too embarrassed if we got caught. But I get off to that one a lot, when you're off on your business trips. All right. Your turn."

"Well," Matt replied, "this is a recent fantasy of mine, but...I want to watch you play with another guy. No one we know, just some guy you think is hot. I want to watch you in the throes of lust, I want to watch your face as another guy makes you come."

"Wow. I'm not sure I'd be up for *that*."

Only the sounds of the road filled the car as Kira conjured the image of a handsome stranger gazing at her with lust-filled eyes.

She broke the silence. "But I admit...the thought of it is kind of hot."

Matt only smiled, satisfied, as if Kira had actually agreed to his fantasy.

"So what shall we do tonight?" Matt asked. "The place we're staying is a college town, so they should have some fun nightlife. How about we go out after dinner, make things a little interesting?"

"Interesting how?" she asked.

"You said you wanted to have sex in public..."

"Whoa, no," she interrupted, turning her body toward him. "I said it was a hot fantasy. That's not the same thing. What are you plotting, Matt?"

Matt didn't reply. He just looked at the road and tapped his fingers on the steering wheel.

"Hmph," she frowned, and slumped back into her seat. She knew she wasn't going to get any more out of him.

As the miles rolled by, Kira racked her brain trying to figure out what Matt had in store for her. But before long her mind began replaying her favorite public-sex fantasy, changing the location to a remote college town on the high plains.

Soon enough, the town, with its historic, snow-topped buildings, approached in the distance, and Kira came back to reality.

"So when are you going to try it out, Matt?" she asked impatiently. Kira waited as a firm-breasted twentysomething in an extra-small football jersey arrived with their drinks, setting a cosmopolitan in front of Kira and a Jack and Coke in front of Matt. When the waitress left Kira continued, "The anticipation is killing me!"

"If I told you, it would spoil the suspense," Matt teased. He felt the remote in his pants pocket, turning it over in his hand, relishing the power he wielded. The power to make someone squirm. The power to make her come. From a distance.

His fingers felt out the buttons. He had memorized their functions from the booklet. Bottom one was LOW, middle was MEDIUM and the top one was HIGH. Pressing HIGH again, the text cautioned, was like turning a guitar amp's dial *past 10—to 11.*

After checking in to their hotel, Kira and Matt had taken

a walk downtown and found a sex shop on a side street. Matt had sprung for a wearable silicone vibrator that promised to get Kira's juices flowing, "anytime, anywhere."

After their late dinner, Kira had run off to the restaurant bathroom to slip the toy inside her jeans for the night ahead. They'd exited onto the cold, icy street, and then ducked into the first bar that looked warm and inviting.

It was Friday, and the largely college-aged crowd was already going full steam, standing three and four deep at the bar, shooting pool in the adjacent room and drinking in groups at the wooden tables around them. Harried young waitresses flew by with bottles of cheap beer, past dusty brick walls holding university pennants, neon liquor signs and faded photos of old football games.

"I don't know how well I can hold my alcohol these days," Kira warned, taking another sip. "And by the way, this drink is strong," she said, her cheeks growing red. "You'd better cut me off after this. I'm getting too old to throw them back."

"You're still younger than me," Matt protested, "so no excuses."

"Yeah, but you don't have the Asian intolerance thing to deal with like I..."

Without warning, Kira let out a short, loud scream, and then froze. Her face was now a warm crimson.

"What happened?" Matt whispered, looking concerned. The noise of the bar absorbed most of her scream, but a couple at the next table over was looking their way.

Kira punched Matt's arm and leaned in close, as if to hide. "I told you to start out slow! What was that, extra high?"

"That was me? Sorry," he apologized. "I must have hit the wrong button." Kira let out a breath and looked back to see the couple had turned toward each other again.

Matt looked into his drink and wondered what had happened. He hadn't pressed anything. His hand was barely touching the remote.

Deciding he should check that it was working properly, his thumb found the bottom button. He took a deep breath, pressed it, and watched for Kira's reaction.

Her glossy pink lips parted and her eyes rose up to the ceiling as low, rolling vibrations massaged her clit, ebbing and flowing in long, delightful waves.

"Mmm," she purred. "That's *much* better. It's like a..."

After just ten seconds, the vibrations stopped again.

"Hey," Kira complained. "Don't stop now, you've just started!"

"*I'm* in control," Matt declared. "I'll decide when you'll get pleasure and when you'll just sit there, aching for me to turn it on again...or turn it up." He smiled wickedly, causing Kira to cross her arms and scrunch her lips together in an exaggerated pout.

Again Kira jumped. This time a shorter, softer yelp escaped her lips.

"You did it again! Listen," she added with a stern look, "if you can't play fair with this we're going back to the hotel. I'm serious."

She delivered the "last chance" look he knew so well and reached for her phone to check for any messages from their sitter.

Matt glanced over at the couple who had eyed them before and caught them looking at him and Kira again. They quickly turned away, the guy reaching for his drink and the girl pretending to write a text on her pink Hello Kitty phone.

Matt studied them more closely this time. They looked to be college students, probably seniors. Wavy, blonde hair fell past the girl's shoulders and a pair of thin-rimmed eyeglasses gave her a smart, studious look. A low-cut, olive-green top showed off her ample cleavage.

Her boyfriend looked like a young Paul Newman, with dark hair and bright blue eyes. One hand held his beer, but Matt noticed him toying with something in his other hand. It almost looked like...

Matt froze.

Through the gaps in his fingers he recognized the curved plastic and the pale blue color. It was a remote—the same kind that controlled the toy he'd bought for his wife. The same toy that was nestled against her clit right now.

Matt realized what was going on. This younger couple was having a little remote toy fun tonight, too. And Kira's vibe was fully in range of their remote.

Had *they* figured it out?

Matt considered what to do while Kira pressed her phone against her ear, trying to listen to a voice mail. They could leave and find another bar, but he didn't know the town and it was freezing outside. But one more stray buzz, and he knew they'd be going to sleep without sex tonight.

Kira interrupted his thoughts. "Kayla checked in, she said everything's fine at home."

The waitress appeared out of nowhere with a tray holding two more drinks. "Oh, we didn't order another round," Matt said, but the waitress set the cocktails in front of them anyway. "Compliments of your friends over there." She gestured with her hand and floated back toward the bar.

Matt and Kira turned their heads in unison. The couple was looking over at them, and this time they didn't turn away. The guy's elbow was on the table and he turned his palm toward them, revealing what was beneath his fingers.

It took Kira only a second to recognize what he was holding and then to grasp that *he*—this unknown college guy in this isolated Montana town—had been buzzing her clit.

Kira turned to Matt with a helpless look, then back to the couple to try to gauge their intent.

The guy seemed relaxed and amused, while the girl looked giddy and animated, whispering things in his ear and smiling mischievously. She turned back toward them, kissed her finger-tips and in a long, slow exhale, blew the kiss toward Kira.

Matt looked for his wife's reaction, and a smile, tenuous but sincere, crept across her lips. She wasn't upset. He breathed a quiet sigh of relief, while the girl decided to push things a little further. Reaching across her boyfriend, she commandeered the remote, set it down in front of her and looked back to Kira.

And then, closing her fist, she extended her index finger and pressed the middle button. Her eyes sparkled as her own vibe started up again, and she looked up at Kira to watch her reaction.

Kira's muscles tensed and her torso rose a few inches before slowly settling back down. She knew she'd better mask her body's responses—they were in public, after all—but these vibrations were stronger, more urgent, more distracting. Her eyes closed and she bit her lower lip.

A minute later the pleasure stopped, and Kira opened her eyes and reawakened to the bar and the activity all around. Seeing all three sets of eyes on her, she blushed, but her cheeks were already red from the drinks.

Satisfied, the girl returned the remote to her boyfriend.

Kira could now barely conceal her impatience. The first, unexpected jolts had been unwelcome, but now she craved vibrations, and stronger ones.

Looking again at the boyfriend—the keeper of the remote—

she picked up her martini glass, put it to her lips and sipped from it slowly, without breaking eye contact.

To anyone watching, her body language said little, but Matt knew better. It said a lot that she hadn't decided to leave or to remove the vibrator. After all, they didn't know this couple, and this guy they'd never met now had a kind of control over Matt's wife that only a small number of former lovers had ever had.

It said even more that she was engaging with them, transmitting her curiosity and arousal across the bar with her eyes. Matt was watching a new, more daring side of his wife.

The guy returned Kira's gaze, his expression matching her poker face as the seconds ticked by.

For Kira, this was new and thrilling. She didn't know him, and probably didn't know anyone who knew him. He could be a philosophy major at the college up the road or a waiter at a bar and grill. All Kira knew was what she saw—a twentysomething with maddeningly rousing, masculine features and an apparent penchant for mischief. Not more handsome than Matt, exactly, but different, mysterious.

All these factors titillated her senses, and made her think about that most provocative body part of the sexy stranger, one she couldn't see. What did it look like? Was it big? Was this making him hard?

Still holding their visual standoff, the guy extended his hand toward the remote, painfully slowly, to provoke her desire all the more. Kira couldn't help breaking eye contact to look at the little plastic controller, the solution to her most urgent, primeval need. She was nearly overflowing with Pavlovian anticipation.

His finger paused, hovering over the middle button as he dramatically considered which level of pleasure to administer to her. The next moment, he punched the button at the top of the remote: HIGH.

Kira's shoulders pressed hard against the back of the booth. Fast and intense, the vibrations raced through her pussy and seemed to reverberate outward to every nerve ending.

Struggling to adapt to the new level of stimulation, her eyes darted around the bar, afraid her expression was as revealing as a wet T-shirt. The buzzing against her clit felt so intense now that she wasn't sure how long she could hold out. She worried she'd soon either come hard and uncontrollably or need to unzip her jeans and pull the vibe right out of her panties.

The girlfriend, on the other hand, must have had practice with her toy; she seemed less aroused by the buzzing beneath her panties than by watching her boyfriend get this shy, black-haired woman off from across the bar.

Instead of turning it off, he let the remote be and crossed his arms, showing Kira that he wasn't going to stop the vibrations to her clit soon.

The next few moments defied time. Kira was vaguely aware of their surroundings: the loud music, boisterous conversations breaking into laughter, warm, dim light. But all that felt like a memory; the only things reaching her immediate awareness were the burning arousal welling up inside her and that penetrating image of the confident, unfamiliar male behind it.

She watched him through a blissful haze, a swirling, levitating sensation that heightened her sensitivity still further and sped her ascent up to a tightening spiral of pleasure. She felt Matt's fingers sliding up her inner thigh, and out of instinct she reached for him under the table, to fill her sudden need for a cock in her hand.

But her muddled mind mixed the feeling of the hardness beneath her husband's slacks with the image of the handsome stranger. Kira suddenly felt, on a visceral level, that it was the stranger's cock in her hand.

This sent a new rush of pleasure to her pussy and the orgasm, which had been hovering so close for so long, began to envelop her. It came on slow but unstoppable, like a two-story wave on the shore rising and curling in slow motion. Her pussy contracted and a flood of ecstasy began to build.

That's when the boyfriend went for broke. He pressed the top button again and the little toy jumped to its highest setting.

Kira's slow-motion film suddenly jerked into fast-forward. Rapid-fire vibrations pulsed through her clit, fast as a strobe light, and in the next heartbeat the wave broke. The orgasm overwhelmed her senses and swept her away, finally leaving her breathless and spent.

Half an hour later, back in their hotel room, clothes strewn across the floor, Kira and Matt collapsed onto the pillows after a frenzied bout of sex.

"That was so...fucking..." Kira panted. "Hot."

"Mmm-hmm," Matt replied. "The whole time we were fucking, I was thinking about what that couple did to you.

"You know," he continued, "between me watching while someone else made you come, and you having an orgasm in public, that little toy pretty much fulfilled both our fantasies tonight."

"Yeah. But don't feel too satisfied yet, Matt." Kira ran her fingertips up his arm. "This was just night one of our trip, and I have a few new fantasies."

PRICKLES

Elizabeth Coldwell

One day, I'll learn my lesson. I'll be mindful that when my Master gives me an instruction, he expects it to be carried out promptly, and if he makes a choice then I must be respectful of it.

This extends to our domestic arrangements, too, for David isn't just my Master: he's also my husband of eighteen months. Not that I'm any kind of downtrodden doormat, trapped in a marriage that's all about getting what *he* wants—far from it. It's just that, sometimes, getting what I want means directly disobeying his wishes.

And that's how I find myself in the position I'm in right now—waiting in the guest bedroom, naked, for David to arrive and give me the punishment I've earned. On the face of it, I only made the smallest of mistakes. When packing his lunch for work this morning, instead of slotting in his usual muesli bar alongside the flask of homemade turkey soup and a crisp Braeburn apple, I added a slice of Christmas cake, wrapped in foil.

Nothing wrong with that, you might think, given we still have almost half the cake that graced the dining table on Christmas night, when my parents and his came over for supper. The newspapers encourage us to be thrifty at this time of year, after all the spending and excesses of the holiday season, so using up the leftovers in David's lunches makes perfect sense. Except that he hates Christmas cake, always has, and sending a piece to work with him can only be viewed as a small but deliberate act of provocation.

He'll have spent the remainder of the afternoon contemplating his response. I wouldn't be at all surprised if he'd left that piece of cake unwrapped on his desk, so every time he looked up from his paperwork it would be there in his sight line, a constant reminder of how I've disappointed him. As for me, I've carried out the housework in a state of squirming anticipation, wondering just what he'll have planned for me on his return.

I won't have to wait much longer to find out; I can hear his tread on the stairs, firm and steady. Every step seems to convey the strength of his purpose, his determination not to be swayed by any pleading or apology on my part. Just the way I love it.

He didn't mention the lunchbox incident, as I've come to think of it, over dinner. We briefly discussed the details of our respective days: his gentle sinking back into the office routine after a week spent at home, my need to get a repairman in to look at our misbehaving washing machine. Beneath this mundane conversation simmered the prospect of the punishment to come: unspoken but undeniable.

At last, when I rose to clear the plates and stack the dishwasher, David said, "Those can wait, Julianne. Go to the guest room, strip and assume the position. I want you ready for me by the time I get up there."

He never has to raise his voice, or bark out an order. The

fact that he makes everything seem like a perfectly reasonable request always adds an extra frisson to his words. Even before I've left the dining room, my pussy has begun to clench with lust and a damp heat suffuses my underwear. I swear that David could make me come with his voice alone, though I've never dared to propose the challenge.

The sheets on the guest bed are clean—I changed them this afternoon—and the room smells faintly of spring-fresh fabric conditioner. David's parents slept here for a couple of nights over Christmas; I'm sure they could have no idea of the games David and I enjoy in here, the domination and submission scenes we act out.

With trembling fingers, I undress, laying my clothes in a neat pile on the bed. When I peel down my panties, there's a tell-tale wetness in the crotch, betraying just how much I want this. We've spent the last few days presenting a sweet, vanilla façade to our families, and now the dark, secret side of us is more than ready to come out and play.

I've no idea how long David will make me wait, naked and facing the wall, my hands linked together at the back of my head. It's a position designed to reinforce my vulnerability, to emphasize what a naughty girl I've been, and yet a fierce excite-ment pulses through me. I need David to see me like this, to admire my willingness to obey, and every moment that passes before he walks through the door only adds to my frustration and growing need.

At last, I hear the door click open and my master enters. His footsteps are muffled by the thick carpet, but I know he is close. Gooseflesh rises on my skin, and I swallow against the sudden obstruction in my throat. He'll be watching me, glancing from my body to the bed to check that I've followed all his instruc-tions, silently counting off any infractions in his head. I don't think I've done anything wrong apart from messing up his lunch, but if he's in the mood, he can always dredge something up to add a little extra to my punishment.

"Turn round," he says, and I do as he asks. Though I try to keep gazing forward, I can't help but drop my eyes to the level of his crotch for a moment, just to gauge the size of the bulge that presses against the front of his dark suit trousers. He hasn't changed out of his office clothes, merely left his jacket hanging over the back of his chair at the dining table, and he looks so gorgeously masculine, with the sleeves of his white shirt rolled up to reveal his solid, lightly haired forearms.

He lets out a little sigh, as if it pains him to be here. "We both know what you've done, Julianne, and exactly why you've done it. You clearly delight in creating little aggravations for me..."

How I love that turn of phrase: it sums up what I've done so beautifully. But then it's no wonder David has a way with words; he's one of the finest editors at his publishing house, after all. It's yet another of the reasons why I'm quite so proud of him. What I love even more is the fact he saves his most cunning acts of creativity for this room, and I'm the only one who gets to experience them.

"I'm sorry, David," I tell him. He's never requested that I call him "Master" or "Sir;" using his first name keeps that quiet tone of domestic discipline on which we both thrive. "I promise I won't make that mistake again."

He regards me for a moment, then shakes his head. "No, you'll just make a different one, won't you? Sometimes it seems there's no limit to the number of simple little things you can get wrong."

His point made, David will now go to fetch tonight's punishment implement from the toy box he keeps hidden in the bottom of the wardrobe. I'm always amazed that no one who's ever stayed here has decided to have a nose around—an impulse that always afflicts me when I'm staying in a strange bedroom—and discovered our secret stash. Maybe the fact that they're stored in a cardboard box that originally contained a pair of calf-length leather boots of mine is why they've gone unnoticed for so long.

Ever since I came upstairs, I've been wondering which of David's selection of whips, paddles, plugs and gags he's intending to use on me. They're all toys he collected over the years before he met me, and he's used them in previous relationships, at play parties and fetish club nights. Sometimes, I think it should bother me that in all the time we've been together he's never bought a new toy especially for me, but it doesn't. Most of his equipment is of the finest quality, the craftsmanship evident in the stitching and the suppleness of the leather. It's all far too nice to be given away or left to rot unused, and I couldn't bear for him not to brandish that cute paddle with the heart-shaped cutouts against my bare bottom. But sometimes I think it would be nice to be surprised for once, for him to reach into that box and withdraw something I've never seen before.

Instead, he surprises me by keeping the door to the wardrobe firmly shut, and keeps on regarding me with that same, faintly disappointed expression. For the first time since I've stepped into the room—indeed, for the first time in longer than I can remember—I have the sense that he's somehow wrong-footed me. Even as my stomach lurches queasily at the thought of David departing from our unwritten script, I can't deny that I like the feeling.

"In the past, I've tried remedying your behavior with all the traditional methods—and none of them have worked." David shakes his head slowly, sadly. "Bare-bottomed spankings, a good old-fashioned six of the best—somehow, Julianne, you remain immune to their corrective effects. So I've decided I will have to try a different tack. And to that end, I'd like you to meet Prickles."

He extends the fist he's kept closed throughout this speech, spreading his fingers to reveal what sits on his palm. I almost want to laugh aloud. He's holding a pink plastic nailbrush in the shape of a hippo. It's one of the toys that fell out of the crackers we pulled at Christmas dinner, and when I'd tidied the table I'd left it on the kitchen windowsill, intending to use it the next time I needed to clean my nails. It seems David has earmarked it for some other purpose.

"I realized," he continues as he steps closer, "that it was high time I introduced you to the concept of sensation play. And Prickles here is going to help you in your initial steps. I'm very interested to see how much of his attention you can take before you beg me to stop—or beg me for more. Your choice."

He smiles, but there's a cruel glitter in his dark eyes. David loves to discipline me, but I can't quite see what he hopes to achieve with the aid of something quite as innocuous as a nailbrush. How on earth could that be any kind of instrument of torment? If he'd brought home one of those pitiless vampire gloves, with the metal points embedded in every finger, points designed to prick and pierce, then I'd have been worried. But David knows my limits, and would never use anything on me that has the capacity to draw blood. So withstanding whatever he thinks he's going to do to me with this silly little brush will be a breeze.

"Ready?" he asks.

My reply is defiant. "Bring it on."

He strokes the brush lightly up my arm, its myriad soft plastic bristles tickling as they go. The sensation is not unpleasant, and I relax into it. I'm so used to being bent over the bed to receive a spanking or a paddling when I've been bad that this feels more like pampering than punishment.

I revise that opinion a little when David begins to concentrate his attentions on my armpit. I'm not exceptionally ticklish, but I can't suppress the shudder that goes through me as he runs the brush back and forth over the delicate skin there. Spotting my reaction, he begins to move Prickles, as he's christened his new toy, in concentrated circles.

I swallow down the whimper that is trying to escape from my lips.

"Had enough yet?" David asks, and I shake my head, determined not to give him the satisfaction of letting him know how much this is already getting to me. "Very well, then..."

He pulls Prickles out of my armpit, and I've barely recovered from its onslaught before he's applying the damned thing to my breast. Again, he moves it in slow circles at first, the bristles caressing me deliciously, like a thousand tiny fingertips. Now, this I could get to like.

David is watching the play of emotions on my face, gauging the exact moment when switching the focus of his strokes to my nipple will have the maximum impact. The little bud has been hard and desperate to be touched almost since the moment David ordered me to go upstairs and undress, and when he begins to flick at it with the nailbrush I can't hold back my response any longer.

"Oh god..." I moan, as the soft to-and-fro motion changes to more of a heavy scrubbing and what started as pure pleasure quickly begins to verge on pain. David has always loved to torment my tits, taking my nipple in his fingers and squeezing until the feeling is almost more than I can stand, and now he's realized he can cause exactly the same reaction with this stupid nailbrush.

"Want me to stop?" he asks. "Because if I do, that's it.

Punishment over. You put your clothes back on, we go downstairs and spend the evening watching TV like none of this ever happened."

That might be an enticing prospect, except I know what he really means by "that's it." I don't get to come, and even though my breasts are mottled red and my nipples swollen and aching from the treatment they've received, my need for orgasm is growing. So, aware that whatever I reply, he'll have the upper hand, I tell him, "No, David, please don't stop."

"Good girl." Those words always cause something to come unglued within me, with their affirmation that my behavior is pleasing him—that *I* am pleasing him. I want to sag against the wall for support, but instead I hold myself upright, staring straight ahead as he draws Prickles over each of my nipples in turn before running the toy down the valley between my breasts.

The brush continues on its downward path, prickling and tickling the skin of my chest and belly. There's only one place its journey can logically end, and already I'm dreading and anticipating that moment in equal measures. I bite my lip as it continues on its inexorable path. Lower...lower...

"Look at me," David orders.

I can't. If our eyes meet, he will be able to see into my soul, and know exactly what he's reduced me to. And yet I have to.

As he sweeps Prickles over my hair-free, sensitive mound, I raise my gaze slightly, to lock with his. There's amusement in his eyes, but admiration, too. Whatever he decides to give me, I will take, however much of an effort it costs me, and he loves me for that.

The brush skims the insides of my thighs, and now its touch is too light. I need more contact, more friction to help the orgasm that's building within me.

"Please..." He said I'd be begging him to stop, or begging

him for more. The word *stop* is a million miles from my lips, even though I don't know what I'll do if he actually presses that wicked, maddening brush between my legs.

The strain of holding my position, fingers linked behind my head, legs wide enough apart to offer him easy access, is beginning to tell. I can feel my thigh muscles burning, and my shoulders ache with the strain of remaining still. But I can ignore these discomforts. All that matters is receiving the pleasure I crave.

David's gaze still bores into mine. I can't hide anything from him. All I can do is whimper helplessly as he skims Prickles over the place where I am wettest and hottest and neediest. Those soft bristles make the barest of contact with my clit, and that's all it takes. Using everything from featherlight touches to harsh rubs, mixing up the sensations until I'm not sure where pleasure ends and pain begins, David has brought me to the point where I'm coming, calling out his name and threatening to topple over, so strong are the waves crashing through me.

He wraps me in his arms and I cling to him: my Master, my rock, my everything.

"Let's go downstairs," he says. I'm aware that he hasn't had his own pleasure yet; the insistent press of his cock against my belly as we cuddle is all the reminder I need of that. We'll be spending the rest of the evening in front of the TV, just as he said, but my head will be in his lap and my mouth will be full of his cock. At this moment, I can't think of any better way to spend my time.

One day I'll learn my lesson. But if a session with Prickles is the consequence of my bad behavior, that day will be a while off yet.

GIFT

Dena Hankins

I recline on the ramp-shaped cushion Margaret made us. She's between my legs on a footstool, lubricating her hands. She rubs the silky white fluid into her skin like lotion.

Her knobby knuckles arrest my attention. They shock me with their girth, every time. I'm fascinated by these strong, delicate, painful hands, practicing a new skill in her late sixties.

Her lips curve as she looks me over. "Ready?"

"I could use a little pillow."

"Of course." She leans to the side slowly, favoring her healing hip. My feet are propped on chairs, extra pillows piled along the arms. I'm quite comfortable and Margaret can reach me without bending or stretching. She offers me a pillow with her lubricated hand and we both laugh. I put the pillow behind my head.

Margaret adds two more pumps of lube into her cupped palm, dips some up and spreads it on my thin pussy lips. Slipping her fingers between them, she feeds moisture to my inner lips, over the hood of my clitoris. I clench a little as she swipes lower.

She presses the lube into my cunt, feeding it with her thumb and then spreading it in and around with her finger. Her skin is slick and soft, her nails too thin and well trimmed to scratch me where I'm tender. She rubs the remaining lube into her hands and then begins pressing, pinching and pulling my labia. "Wake up," she murmurs. When I laugh, she glances up with that devilish grin. Oh, how I love the way she looks at me!

This therapeutic exercise brings fresh blood and lymph into the tissues of my vulva. Push out the old, let the new flow in. The deep pressing and rubbing of her finger in my pussy wakes my circulatory system, but it lights my libido as well. Margaret's wonderful hands bring my nerve endings to life. The charms of spontaneous lubrication pale compared to the focused attention of this ritual. Stroking, stretching, Margaret sees my clitoris emerge from its swaddling clothes. I know she sees this, because she adds a second finger inside me. Oh yes.

Concentration sharpens her features toward severity, the lines beside her eyes and down her cheeks deepening, her lips tight. She hungers to watch me come alive under her hands and she will tolerate no interruptions.

The two fingers in me bend together, sweeping from side to side with a twist of her wrist. She strokes the long legs of my clitoris from inside, left and then right, repeating this and stretching the skin between the back of my cunt and the pucker of my butthole. Patience, patience.

She adds more lube and thrusts.

"Oooohhh, yes," I croon. I pull up with my PC muscles, sucking her hand closer, and then relax. When her arm flexes to force her fingers farther in, her large, soft breasts plump over the lace-edged bra. The rolled-up sleeves of her chenille robe brush the insides of my thighs.

The large knuckles of her fingers pop into me and, yes, the

shock runs through me like an awakening. If she were to try this before the lube and massage, I wouldn't be soft enough to stretch for her. I pant my gratitude. "Yes, that's perfect. You know exactly…"

She pulls her knuckles against my clenching muscles, lets her fingers ease into me, then tugs outward again. I tighten to keep her inside where she presses above and behind the legs of my clit. I'm amazed she can do this with her arthritis. I breathe deeply and dig my heels into the cushions to raise my hips.

Margaret twists in her chair to grab the small vibrator from its warm lube bath. It is waterproof, short and flat and as wide as three of my fingers. Its gentle curve rests in her palm easily and she can manipulate it without grasping, crucial to our enjoyment since her arthritis makes it hard to grip something buzzing.

Everything is warm and clean and easy to reach. She prepares my house for our trysts, setting up the cushions and pillows, ensuring that lubricant and toys will be close at hand. The first time she used the double boiler to warm lube, I laughed. Now I bow to her domestic expertise.

She can't bend forward far enough to touch my breasts, so she tells me what she wants to see. "Press your breasts together, Helen. Mound them on your ribs and pinch your nipples for me." Her eyes track my hands over my belly and up to push my breasts together. One nipple tightens slowly, but the other lies flat, almost concave in the loose flesh of my smallish breast. The hum of the vibrator curves my lips with anticipation and then I laugh. Both nipples poke up, hard as can be. "They know how much you like this," she says.

"I do like it. You give me so much pleasure, Margaret." She doesn't argue, modesty displaced by her fascination with my clitoris. She craves my excitement and can spend hours making my pussy soft and wet and my clit hard and needy. She had never seen her own clit when she answered my personal ad for a mature woman interested in exploring lesbian sex with an inexperienced woman in her seventies. Though we've rectified that, she gets more pleasure out of mine than her own, it seems.

Margaret lays the vibrator against the back of her hand. The knuckles that rub me inside now buzz softly against excited tissue. I moan and let the sensation come. I don't have to work for this. She will take care of me.

She shifts the vibrator and presses its long edge between my inner and outer labia. She licks her lips. "You are so beautiful, Helen."

I am still holding my breasts high and I look over them at my lover. "I feel beautiful, Margaret." Scars and wrinkles, loose flesh and gray hair. These don't disappear between us. We see each other with clear eyes, clear enough to catch the flush of arousal and the engorgement of lips and the heaviness of eyes. Clear enough to love the soft delicacy of each other's secret skin and the hard insistence of bone under thin skin.

The warm, slick vibrator transits my vulva, around and around, jolting me when it slips inside a tiny bit along with her fingers. "Oh, that's amazing." Margaret's concentration has eased. She's confident I will reach orgasm today. She has led me through the gate between feeling good and feeling urgent and I'm prepared to let her take me deep.

Finally, the vibrator slips up and covers my clit. With an easy rocking of her hand, a motion she can keep up for hours, Margaret gives me the side-to-side motion that makes my inner muscles pick up the rhythm. I rock my hips with her, just a little, and she moans now. Her rosy face relaxes. Her lips are bigger and damp from being licked and bitten in her deep concentration, but also from her own excitement in this sex we're having.

One end of the vibrator is pointier than the other and she begins to roll the point under my clitoris on each rock from side to side. It slides the hood back and puts the vibration directly on the tender tip, which makes me jerk on each pass. My repeated *oh*s start as breath and build until I'm panting between each cry.

Margaret pumps her fingers into me slowly, in delicious rhythm with the rocking and tipping of the vibrator. The fingers that are not in me slip along the bit of skin that leads to my tight pucker and give the lightest rubbing there. I start to lose track of what she is doing in the wash of sensation and know that I am getting closer.

"Pinch them, Helen." She's right, and I obey without thinking, twisting and rolling my nipples between my fingers. Margaret leans in and takes a gentle bite of the inside of my thigh. I jerk and twitch and wrap my mind and body around this glorious woman, breathing heavily with the work we're doing together. When I focus on her face, she holds my eyes and I simply float to her. A look like a kiss, a touch like glad weeping, and Margaret grinds the vibrator into my clit to shove me over the edge.

Crying out, I writhe, muscles throughout my body stretching to accommodate my pleasure. Margaret doesn't stop. She craves this so strongly that she drags more and more from me. My eyes never leave hers and she shakes with the effort of wringing every last tremor from me.

Finally, emptied, I release my reddened breasts and put a hand over hers, her hand that still rocks the vibrator against me. She stills and sighs, her flushed chest rising and falling. She turns off the vibrator with one trembling hand and grips my fingers in hers.

I can tell that my pussy has absorbed most of the lube, but she knows it too. She leans forward far enough to kiss my finger-tips and lets my hand fall. One last pump of lubricant hits her fingers and she eases it over my fattened labia and shy clitoris. She presses the lube between her fingers and my delicate tissues so that she can pull her knuckles out of me without pain.

I sigh at the long, slow slide of her withdrawal. She's still focused on my pleasure, making me feel good even with these last caresses. "I'm the luckiest woman in the world," I say. It's only truth and the truth is worth telling. But Margaret is already hiding, like my clitoris, from the glorious intensity of what we've done. So complicated, this woman of my desiring.

Margaret came to me untutored. She had never had an orgasm, nor had she ever given one from her own actions and efforts. She answered my ad from a need for touch, a hunger for physical contact, and she imagined two women doing little more than cuddling. Her road to orgasm was both long and short— thirty-some years of marriage but only weeks of seeing me.

She loves what she does to me, but she still feels that what we do is foreign, strange, though full of pleasure for us both. We have become best friends, which we both enjoy. The erotic element brings us closer, but I'm not certain she will allow it to blossom into romance. A woman can hope.

I bring my legs together and sit up. We kiss, lips pressing and sliding, and rub our soft cheeks together. I put my hand to the nape of her neck and rest my forehead on her shoulder.

After a moment, we stand and she helps me on with my robe. In the kitchen, Margaret washes her hands and pulls out the plate she had prepared before we began. Fruit, cheese and crackers, with a radish rose in the middle. I kiss her cheek in thanks and she pats my shoulder. She pours us each glasses of mixed fruit juice and we sit together.

"My daughter has done it again." Margaret turns her glass between her hands.

My mouth full of dill havarti, I cock my head in question.

"She changed my doctor's appointment without speaking with me first. It just infuriates me when Jill behaves as though I'm a child."

I swallow. "She was going to drive you?"

"Yes, but the senior center's bus could have taken me. Or I could have rescheduled the appointment myself."

My heart twinges a little that she doesn't consider the option of asking me to drive her.

She sighs. "Breaking my hip was the worst thing that has ever happened to me. I hate living with Jill. She can't stop taking care of me but she never asks what I want. She didn't even let me go through my own furniture."

An old complaint. While Margaret recuperated from the broken hip in the rehab facility, Jill talked her into selling the family home and moving into Jill's condo. Jill is an efficient woman, a CPA, and by the time Margaret was discharged, the house and most of the furnishings had been sold.

"I'd say you could use a little more respect along with the love." I pop a grape into my mouth to force myself to stop there.

Margaret makes a cheddar and wheat cracker sandwich. "I'd agree. My rehab is going extraordinarily well. My therapist is amazed by my progress. Getting in here is a snap." My house is a test of her healing and balance, with five steps to both the front and back doors and an uneven path leading from the driveway to the house.

"It must be all the healthy blood flow to your pelvic region."

Margaret giggles, blushing. "And the regular stretching."

"To regular stretching." I tap my juice glass to hers and drain it. We'll have wine later, but I want to be clearheaded for the next part of our day together. "I have a present for you."

Margaret looks up from sliding the leftover cheese into Ziploc bags. "Really? What is it?"

"Come see."

A smile lightens the curves of her cheeks. "Sounds good to me."

I rinse the glasses and put away the crackers while she finishes storing the cheese. Taking her hand in mine, I lead her back to my bedroom. I strip and slip her robe from her shoulders to drape at her waist and step behind her to unhook her bra. With a kiss for the red mark on each shoulder, I slide the straps down her arms and let the bra fall to the floor. I wrap my arms around her from the back, under her heavy breasts, and squeeze. She moans at the contact of skin on skin and releases the belt of her robe. She shoves it down and then pushes down her panties as well. She always wants more skin.

I finish the job of nudging her panties to her feet and then wrap myself around her again, her back to my front, touching from my cheek by her ear to our ankle bones pressing lightly together. One arm circles her soft belly and the other raises and supports her breasts. She is a glorious armful of flesh and I moan now, softly, my hot breath on her earlobe.

"Where is my present?" Margaret's voice is husky.

"Not just yet."

I bid her to lie down and sit next to her on the bed, cross-legged. I lubricate my hand and her pussy in much the same way she did for me earlier. She would love to spread her legs wide, but the broken hip is too stiff. I prepare her, wetting her thoroughly for the friction she loves. "Wake up," I say, mimicking her voice. Margaret laughs and her muscles jump against my fingertips.

After her labia darken and plump, she pulls at my shoulder, moaning. I roll on top of her, one leg between hers, and pull one of her breasts up to fill both my hands. I bite her nipple and press it hard against the roof of my mouth with my tongue. She runs her hands over my shoulders and into my hair, lightly holding my head in place. The lube I filled her with spreads across my thigh and I rub as best I can. I pull back, gasping, and we arrange a low ramp to raise her hips and plenty of support for her legs.

Now I can rise up on my knees and rub her whole vulva with my thigh. I bounce against her and she groans. I know she wants more. We've talked about it. She wants me to lie on top of her, to penetrate her and rub her clitoris, all at the same time. I lie forward, resting my torso on her belly and bringing her breasts up to pillow my head. Almost there. So close to what she wants, but I have never yet been able to penetrate her while doing this.

I grind my thigh on her pussy and raise my head. Her head is thrown back, the flesh of her cheeks flowing away from her open mouth. "Are you ready for your present?" My question penetrates her slowly and she breathes deeply before nodding. "Stay here," I say, "and keep your eyes closed."

She does both, but her hands follow me as I push back from her. They fall, landing on her belly, and I know how I will keep her busy while I prepare.

"Bite your nipple," I say. "Bring it to your mouth and do what you love me to do." Her breasts are large and malleable. The nipple can easily reach her mouth and she uses both hands to bring it up. She bites, harder than I dare, and tugs with a fierce motion of her head.

I pull the thigh harness from my top drawer, along with the red-and-black-swirled silicone dildo. A young woman at the sex toy shop helped me work out a plan to accommodate her stiff hip and fulfill her desires. I glance at Margaret and groan.

"You are so sexy, Margaret." She has taken the initiative and is touching her clitoris. Still holding one breast and gnawing on her nipple, she has added a slow circling.

"Is my present almost ready?" Her wet nipple gleams, distended from its rough treatment. The flesh of her breast overflows her grasping hand and I want to squeeze it in my own.

"Nearly there," I answer, hoping it's true. The Velcro releases with a loud rasp and she frowns, eyes still closed. I shove the colorful dildo between the neoprene band and the rubber O-ring, like a huge thread in a giant needle. Balls and a defined head present a very lifelike shape, though the color distorts that aspect of its appearance. With the wide strip of neoprene wrapped around my thigh, the dildo points upward.

"I'm coming back now," I say. Nerves race in my belly. I slide onto the bed, kneeling between her legs. I let her feel my unadorned thigh beside hers and stroke a hand from her sternum to her pubic bone. The touch makes her sigh and I lean over her. The thigh harness rubs between her legs and the dildo taps her pubic bone.

"I would like to fuck you now, Margaret. May I?"

"Yes, please." She reaches down to stroke my thigh. "Is it time to open my eyes?"

"Not yet." I imagine she thinks I've purchased a new vibrator. "Wait for it."

"As you like, Helen." She settles in with those words. I sense her willingness, her openness. Her trust is such a lovely gift.

After lubricating the dildo thoroughly, I press it gently against the opening of her vagina. She hums in the back of her throat and I move my knee forward a little. Leaning over her shoves the dildo deeper and Margaret twitches. Of course she can tell that my thigh is between her legs, but she doesn't yet know that I am guiding the toy that way.

I lean closer and, slowly, give her all of what she wants. In and out, deeper and out again, until we are breast to breast, belly to belly. I shove my arms under her shoulders and say, "You can open your eyes now."

She blinks and asks, "What on earth is that?"

I laugh a little hoarsely. "It's a thigh harness and dildo."

"What?" she repeats.

"What do you think of it?"

Her eyes are wide and she is breathing heavily. "It's wonderful."

"Let's see if we can make it even better."

She sucks my lips, caressing them with her tongue. I bite her lower lip and then shift down and back up again. I can't tell what is happening very well, but she responds with a shudder. Her arms wrap around me and I use her shoulders as leverage to thrust into her harder. I slowly get a feeling for the resistance against the dildo and harness. A pull when I slide it out of her cunt and a push when I slide it back in. I can tell she likes it best when I'm all the way in, so I shorten the stroke and shove hard against her when I'm all the way in.

Her shiver rubs her against the dildo and harness. She moans and I rock my thigh from side to side. Margaret's belly pushes out against me in her attempt to arch her hips and I grab the sheets for stability. My forearms squeeze the soft sides of her abundant breasts and she looks up at me, eyes wide.

"Helen, this is amazing. I can feel you everywhere."

I nip at her lower lip again and then sink into a deep, deep kiss. Slowly, and then faster, Margaret and I rock and press, pull and push. Her frantic breathing sweetens the air and sweat dampens the hair around her face. She has never moved so much, so recklessly.

Margaret arches and takes me by surprise. She rolls over

with me and cries out when the dildo leaves her body. Reaching between us, she guides it back in, lying heavily on top of me. She covers my chin and neck with kisses, lower on my body than a moment ago, and I lie still in shock. My formerly demure lover surrounds me with flesh and hunger, rubbing herself on me. She uses my shoulders to pull herself up before slamming back down on the dildo. My hands go to her back, and I hope there's enough lubrication for this wild thrusting.

She rubs hard, with short, sharp motions, jostling me over and over. I squeeze her nipples hard, and she falls on me. Her hands rush from my head to my shoulders and down to my hips. Her weight presses me hard into the bed and I'm dazed by the voraciousness of her need.

Margaret grips my behind, lifting me into her so that her thigh grinds my clit when she pulls off the dildo and then disappears when she slams back down. I stuff a pillow under my hips to help keep me higher, where she wants me. "Pound your cunt on me," I demand and Margaret growls. I squirm, adding the last tweak to the way her thigh slides on my clitoris.

I come first, vaguely, then more strongly when she doesn't stop. I don't know if I've come again and again or simply kept coming, but my head fills with noise. Margaret pushes up on her hands, grinding herself to a groaning, shivering orgasm. I watch in awe the earthquake that overtakes Margaret's fleshy body.

She collapses and rolls onto the bed next to me. She laughs, gasping for breath, and I grab her hand.

"How are you feeling?" I ask the question tenderly, drawing my finger across the tooth marks Margaret left around her nipple.

"Like an animal. All body and no mind."

I laugh and kiss the mauled nipple.

"A happy animal." She looks down at our bodies. We are lying naked, lube stains everywhere and the thigh harness holding the dildo to my thigh. "I love having so much to rub against." She places a fingertip on the end of the dildo. "Thank you."

"I'm so glad it worked out."

"It did, but it's not just this." My heart contracts in hope at the warmth on her face. "You've given me patience and joy and knowledge and desire. You have given me all the greatest gifts."

"Margaret, you are the gift."

GET YOUR ROCKS OFF

Jocelyn Dex

Vera swiped a strand of hair from her sweaty forehead, laughing when she looked at her filthy, gloved hands. In addition to sweat, she was certain her forehead now sported a gritty streak of dirt.

Since she loved the outdoors and gardening, spring was her favorite time of year. Surveying the newly planted flowers and vegetable plants, she stretched her tired muscles. Just as she pushed up from the ground, her husband's car pulled into the driveway.

Damn, it was already six? She'd been digging in the dirt longer than she'd thought. He waved to her as he got out of the car and walked toward her. She loved the way his suit made him look all professional-businessman-like, but she preferred him in shorts and a T-shirt or naked. Definitely naked. She couldn't get enough of his strong legs, tight butt and muscular shoulders—oh, how she was a sucker for those shoulders. She could never resist sinking her teeth into them when they sexed each other up, if the position allowed for it.

"Hey there." Kane surveyed her disheveled state, smirking. "Lookin' good."

"Very funny."

He brushed the dirt from her face and planted a light kiss on her cheek before looking around the yard. "You've been busy. Looks great."

"Wait until you see the backyard." She couldn't keep the excitement from her voice. "All the tomatoes, cucumbers, jalapeños and zucchini are in the ground."

A smile lit his handsome face, the sun enhancing the natural coppery highlights in his otherwise dark hair. "You're so hot when you get going about your garden."

She snorted as she indicated her dirt-stained clothes with a wave of her hand. "Yeah, this is hotness, all right."

His chocolate-colored eyes darkened as he wrapped an arm around her waist and pulled her against him.

She tried to ward him off. "Ew, I'll get you dirty."

"I like dirty. C'mon. Let's take this inside." Once inside, he grasped the hem of her tank top and whipped it over her head. A frisky glint shone in his eyes as he appraised her naked breasts. "Why don't you clean up and relax with a hot bath?"

"I thought you liked it dirty," she teased.

His husky laugh was like a caress on her skin, making her bare nipples peak. There was no doubt in her mind that her husband was feeling frisky. "Different kind of dirty."

"Okay, but I'll just take a quick shower."

"Nope." He bopped her nose with his forefinger. "I insist. Hot bath. Take your time."

"What're you up to?" When he folded his arms across his chest and gave her a mock-stern look, she saluted him, said, "Yes, Sir," and headed to the bathroom.

Once the tub was filled, she stepped in and sank down. Ah, her husband was a saint for insisting she take her time to relax. Her muscles ached from all the digging, planting, bending and stooping and she melted in the heavenly, hot water.

She took her time cleansing her skin with her favorite coconut bath gel, the fragrance reminding her of the tropical island she and her husband had honeymooned on. They'd been naked most of the time, couldn't keep their hands off each other. Lying back, she closed her eyes and enjoyed the memory.

"Hey, sleepyhead," Kane's husky voice called to her. "You're going to turn into a prune."

Opening her eyes, she saw him perched on the side of the tub, gazing intently at her nakedness. He wore nothing but deep-blue boxer briefs. Busy admiring his physique, it took her a minute to realize the water was lukewarm at best. "How long have I been in here?"

"About forty-five minutes."

She checked her fingers. Yep. Prunes. "Sorry. I didn't mean to be in here so long. Must have dozed off."

He stood, grabbed her favorite thick, daisy-yellow towel and held out his hand to her. When she grasped it, he pulled her to standing and dried her from head to toe, then wrapped the towel around her.

She loved the special attention but wondered to what she owed the pleasure. "What're you up to?" she asked again.

"Can't I take care of my wife?" When she gave him the sideways slant-eye, he laughed and said, "Follow me."

The answer greeted her when she stepped into the bedroom. He'd pulled the blackout shades so the room was dark except for the ten or so white candles, their flames flickering on nightstands on either side of the bed. "Wow. Romantic. Wait. Is that a Crock-Pot on the nightstand?"

He chuckled. "Ignore that for now. Go ahead, lie down on the bed. Get comfortable."

She climbed onto the bed and started to lie down on her back but he stopped her. "Drop the towel and lie on your stomach."

She couldn't keep the grin and giggle to herself. Her husband wasn't usually so director-like in the bedroom. "What's going on?"

"Eh." He twirled his finger, motioning her to flip over.

"Okay." She did as requested, butterflies flitting in her stomach, excited about what was to come.

He shucked out of his boxer briefs. Her mouth watered at the sight of his hard cock and she hoped whatever he had planned included it. Sitting beside her on the bed, he picked up a bottle of massage oil, squeezed a generous amount into his left palm and rubbed his hands together vigorously before settling them on her shoulders.

The oil smelled fantastic and the more she breathed the lavender scent, the more her mind relaxed. His strong hands kneaded her shoulders, his thumbs digging in beneath her shoulder blades—not too hard, not too soft, just right, in fact—working out the knots caused by the day's gardening.

"Mmm," she moaned into the pillow.

"Feel good?"

"Mmm-hmm."

His thumbs ran up the base of her neck to her hairline, then back down again. God it felt good. She hadn't realized how much her body needed this. He continued the ministrations, making his way down her back, his oiled hands sliding easily across her freshly cleaned skin. His thumbs circled her sacrum with varying pressure. Vera was surprised when little sparks of arousal shot straight to her pussy. She hadn't known that was an erogenous zone.

With each stroke of his magical fingers, her body both relaxed and came alive at the same time. He varied the pressure, sometimes using featherlight strokes that made her shiver, sometimes digging in deep to undo little knots. All of it made Vera moan, made her want more, her body putty in his masterful hands. When he expertly kneaded her asscheeks, his fingers dipping low between her legs, more tingles shot to her pussy, the moisture of arousal quickly following.

Disappointed when his hands left her body, she turned her head to the side to see what he was up to. He opened the Crock-Pot-looking thing and pulled out a flat, round, gray...rock? "What's that?"

He just smiled. "Relax."

She tensed when he placed the rock on her sacrum, the heat frightening her at first, but she relaxed when the warmth penetrated her skin, seeped into her. It was intense but didn't burn.

He repositioned himself so his legs straddled her upper thighs. The mild roughness of the hair on his legs added a pleasant, contrasting sensation. Taking another rock from the heating unit, he slid the stones up and down her back, her neck, across her shoulders. She thought her muscles would melt from the feeling. Absolutely wonderful. When leaning forward to move the stones higher, his erect cock met with her asscrack, making her want more than the sensual massage. She raised her butt as much as possible in her restricted position, longing for the contact, trying to entice him to do more.

"Stop it." A light smack stung her buttcheek. "I'm not ready for that yet."

"You *feel* ready to me."

"Uh-uh. Just relax."

Leaving one stone at the base of her neck, he moved the other down her spine, teasing the dimple between her cheeks before smoothing it lower and circling her sensitive pucker. Hot sparks of pleasure shot straight to her clit, engorging it, making it weep for attention.

"Should I fuck you here?" Kane's desire-laden voice sent shivers up her spine.

She arched her ass in invitation. "Do it. I need you inside me now."

"Hmm." He reached lower with his other hand, his fingers tracing her wet pussy lips. Sparks shot through her when he slipped inside, finger-fucking her. First with one finger, then with two. "But your pussy's so wet for me. I'll fuck you here first...but not yet." She howled in protest when he pulled his fingers out, leaving her empty again. Moving to her side, he removed the stones from her back. "Flip over."

Although frustrated he hadn't ravaged her, she was eager to see what came next. He pulled her legs over his thighs, spreading her wide, her pussy completely open to him, and she prayed he'd give it more attention soon. The pressure, the need to climax, ate at her, made her restless.

Coating his hands with more oil, he lightly traced his fingers across her neck, over her breasts and down her abdomen. The teasing, featherlight touch left tingles in its wake. Her nipples beaded; goose bumps pricked her skin. He cupped her breasts, coating them with the oil, rolling her nipples between thumb and forefinger.

"Mmm. What did I do to deserve this?"

"I just want to touch you. You like?"

"You know I do. Don't stop."

After coating the rest of her front with the oil, he reached over and pulled two new stones from the heating unit and swirled them around her breasts. The heat and smooth texture gliding over her skin shot another wave of desire to her cunt.

His touch drove her nuts, her body ready, needy, every nerve ending twitchy. She arched her hips upward, trying to make contact with her husband's erection, but he ignored her efforts and continued rubbing her down, heating her skin.

On the next pass down her abdomen, he continued the downward descent, smoothing the rock past her belly button, across the small patch of curls and through her wet slit. Her hips bucked. The heat from the rock meeting with her already hot cunt made her quiver. When he pressed it against her swollen clit, rubbing it with quick, short strokes, she almost came undone.

"Now, Kane," she breathed. "I need you inside me."

His resolve finally broke. Lust burned in his eyes. "Flip over. Get on your knees."

Vera complied. Facedown, ass up, totally vulnerable to him.

He grabbed two handfuls of her asscheeks and spread them apart. "You look so fucking sexy like this." She gasped when he bent and licked her from clit to asshole. "I can't decide whether to fuck you or eat you."

Either of those actions sounded good to her, but desperation to have him inside her won out. "Fuck me. Hurry."

She whimpered and fisted the sheet when he rubbed the head of his cock through her drenched slit, the anticipation making her crazy. He tortured her, teasing her with the delicious friction for long seconds that felt like minutes.

They both cried out when he finally thrust inside. He slammed into her, deep and hard, relentless—just the way she needed. She rocked back as he slammed forward, her cunt swallowing every inch he gave.

He groaned and slowed the pace. Hot rock in hand, he brought it around to her pussy, swirling it in quick, tight circles on her throbbing clit. He'd already revved her up and her body needed release.

The fullness in her pussy, Kane's frenzied thrusts, his animalistic grunts and the heat from the rock on her clit hurdled her toward the edge. Her senses were overwhelmed with panting breaths, the smack of skin slapping against skin, Kane's sweat rolling down her asscheeks, the scent of sex and lavender permeating the air.

One more deep thrust, one more swipe of the rock on her knotted bundle of nerves, threw her into ecstasy. Tendrils of blinding white heat burst from her clit, speared her veins and muscles, shattered her soul.

Kane wasn't far behind. His cock swelled and on one last, deep thrust, his fingers dug into her hips, body twitching as his semen spurted inside her, filling her, warming her insides. He shuddered each time her pussy spasmed around his cock until he was spent and slumped over her, his hot breath tickling her shoulder.

They collapsed to their sides, hearts pounding, and lay there curled into each other until they regained their breath.

She'd never known that kind of pleasure until Kane. He'd always been tuned in to her body, knew when to give, when to take, just how to touch her to make her come apart.

"Wow," she breathed. "After eight years, you still surprise me."

"I try." His fingers traced circles on her shoulder. "Does that mean the rocks were a good buy?"

"*Great* buy." Vera turned to him and teased his bottom lip with her tongue. "But next time, it's your turn."

"Mmm. No argument here." He leaned in and devoured her mouth in a soul-searing kiss. When he broke away, she was breathless and ready for more.

"So, what are you waiting for?"

BYRD AND
THE BEES

Kamala St. Deeds

Tell me, Byrd, why you're suddenly fancying picnics?" Vivian
struggled in her full skirts to keep up with Byrd's long stride
as he crested the wooded hill.

"An experiment, my dear." He wore a smile that reached
more of the left side of his face than his right, which meant he
was up to something. Vivian felt a surge of heat between her
thighs. Whatever he plotted now would surely end up as some
sexual adventure for the two of them, if past experience was
anything to go by.

Her laugh tinkled like music as she took a peek in the basket.
"I see a blanket. I see a bit of oil, and I see something suspi-
ciously shaped..." She withdrew a ceramic something. About
eight inches long and round enough so her thumb and forefinger
just touched. Domed at the top, or was that the bottom? The
other end held a cork with small tubes sticking out of it that
could do more that trickle water. "Like a phallus?"

She drew it out and waggled in front of Byrd. She gripped the sculpture, pretending it was him. "It's even smooth." Some sort of resin had sealed it, strengthening it. "What are you planning, my wicked man?"

Wiggling his eyebrows at her, he said, "My reading last week took me somewhere interesting." He let out a puff of smoke from his pipe.

"Interesting?" She mentally cataloged the books he'd brought home in the past month. "The Vedas?" But even as she asked the question, she could feel him frowning. Their translation had only just begun.

"Caesar's notes of Egyptian practices," Byrd said.

"I take it we're not talking farming?" she asked. She arched her brow and did her best to look coy.

"Well maybe a little ploughing." He laughed and continued onward, leaving Vivian with the ceramic penis, for lack of a better word. He pulled an object out of his pocket and tossed it to her. A quartz crystal: double pointed and six sided, it was an excellent way of storing one's energy.

"Thinking of bottling your sexual energy?" she asked, studying the crystal's perfection. "You could start wars with that."

"Something like that." There was that smile again.

As she walked she looked the cylinder over. She shook it: nothing inside. She pulled out the cork to make sure. The cork still baffled her. Why the tubes? Lost in thought over the mechanics of what Byrd had made, she failed to see him stop. He grabbed her arm.

"Careful now." He pointed up. A faint buzzing met her ears before she spotted the hive hanging from a low branch. "We need just one more thing."

She breathed a sigh of relief. She would have walked into the beehive if he hadn't pulled her back. She took another step back. Never did like bees.

Byrd, however, took a step forward, relieving her of the ceramic penis and crystal as he did. He let the crystal slide inside it. He crept slowly, so sly the bees didn't take him for a threat. Vivian's throat leapt into her mouth, making her gag. He puffed a large cloud of smoke at the hive. He positioned the bottom of the sculpture against the hole the bees used to get in and out of the hive. Then he gave the hive a good hard whack.

The air filled with the sound of angry bees as they flew out of their hive to defend their queen, and right into the hollow part of the ceramic.

"Cork." Byrd swung his hand back toward her.

She couldn't move. She shook her head.

"It's two steps. Won't let them hurt you." He looked at her, his confident blue eyes shining, his fingers outstretched.

She took a step, then another. They were tiny little steps but they were enough to bridge the distance between them and she let the cork fall into his palm.

He stoppered it with grace as he ducked out of the way of a few remaining bees that darted into the air without any clear plan of attack. As they did, she clung to Byrd and he put his strong arm around her. The bees swung about in figure eights before retreating back into their home. Not a one bothered either of them. But why did she feel they were still buzzing all about her?

"Why would you do that?" she asked, her voice too high to be as quiet as she'd hoped.

He smiled, his eyes sparking with desire. "Feel." He wrapped her fingers around the ceramic sculpture. The bees inside made the thing vibrate.

She took her hands away, too quickly. The bees were buzzing all around her, just contained in that thing. "I don't understand. I thought it was for...playing with later."

"It is." He ran his hand down her side, and pulled her close to him. She felt his excitement through his trousers. "Rumors exist of Egyptian women putting bees in gourds for pleasuring themselves. Some even say the Queen Cleopatra invented such things."

"For what purpose?" She looked at the sculpture like it was an alien life form. "How can bees be pleasing?"

"Let me show you," he whispered in her ear. He proceeded to nibble his way down from earlobe to chin. "Let me give you a queen's pleasure."

A queen's pleasure? she thought. The idea of it made her light-headed, or was that her fear of the bees themselves? "But the bees!"

"Only a catalyst, my love." He held up a finger for her to be still. He stepped to the side and brought his mouth to the small tubes inside the cork and exhaled smoke into the tube. He uncorked it and the last bees crawled out, flying to rejoin their hive. "The crystal will resonate with their energy for an hour or more." He brought his arm around her waist. "You are my queen. Allow me to give you this." Byrd's voice grew husky as he laid the ceramic sculpture full of bee buzz between her breasts.

She gasped, in both fear and surprise. As Byrd moved the object over her breast she felt her nipple harden in response, her undergarments moistening. She clutched his muscled arm but thought of nothing to say. She no longer had an objection. A soft moan escaped her lips, which he took for a yes.

He took the ceramic object away, leaving her feeling decidedly unsatisfied. Byrd led her a few steps to a grassy area and quickly laid down a blanket. He beckoned to her. They lay side by side. In one hand he undid the lacing of her top and with the other he controlled the vibrating phallus. He brought out one breast, freeing it from her clothing, and finished pulling at the silk lacing with his teeth, caught somewhere in between being a gentle lover and getting frustrated enough to be tempted to rip them off. Vivian had felt him like this before and she knew the signs. She brought her other breast out herself and wiggled out of her undergarments. This dress had cost too much for him to get too wild with her today.

He rolled the phallus across her breasts, moving the tip in slow circles around her taut nipple. After he teased it with the buzzing contraption, he'd take it away and lower his mouth, using the same motions with his tongue. Her breath came in heaving gasps as the phallus's vibrations heightened her arousal. Every lick brought her closer to her peak.

She tangled her fingers in his silky hair as he worked his way inch by inch over her breasts. She reached down with her other hand and wormed it between the small gap of his clothing, past the curly hairs, finding him, and with delicate touches made him moan.

He shifted so the phallus vibrated first upon her chest, moving slowly on to her stomach, then sliding over her skirts. She lost the buzzing sensation for a moment before she felt the object on her thigh, moving upward until Byrd laid it between her legs, upon her most sensitive area.

She sucked in air as she realized she had not fully grown accustomed to the buzzing upon her flesh. Upon her skin, perhaps, but there? She thought of the bees. Angry bees close enough she could feel their anger. "I can't," she panted. "Bees. Inside. I can't."

"Remember, they are not there, only their vibrations," he whispered, but he moved it up only a quarter inch, to that spot not quite inside that made her wet with pleasure when he ran over it with his fingers or his tongue. He pressed it there, making the buzzing intense enough that she felt it throughout her body.

She moaned, louder than she ever had before. But they were alone out here and it did not matter.

She gripped him, no longer delicate in her movements, wanting to vibrate him with her hand so he could know how this felt. He grunted into her breasts as he continued licking at her nipple, suckling it once, then flicking it with his tongue. And all the while, the vibrations of the bee-infused phallus sent her heat below and flushed her cheeks with pleasure. She let out a groan as she felt the convulsions come, both from her body and from Byrd's as he spouted his climax on her hand. He dropped the container and felt for her with his fingers.

"How was that, my queen?" Byrd asked, sitting up to kiss her. He lingered there, letting his tongue tantalize her lips.

"I've never felt its like," she said. "But I do not have a queen's courage to put such a thing inside."

"They are not there. Only their energy. But I know you too well to think you do not have the courage of a queen." He had that half smile again. "And bees shall be prevalent through the summer."

"All through the summer?" she asked. She shivered at the thought of having the buzzing sculpture near her again, or even, eventually, inside her.

"Plentiful, every single day, so the astrologers predict this year."

"So, many picnics then?" she said.

"Every single day."

THE SECRET SHOPPER

Kitten Boheme

Astrid opened up her email; her heart skipped a beat when she saw one new notification from *him*. Master Markus only emailed her when he had implicit instructions for her to carry out. She simultaneously dreaded and anticipated these emails, anxiously wondering what new task he had devised for her, what new way he wanted her to please him. She stared nervously at the unopened email, her palms beginning to sweat. She took a steadying breath and double-clicked her mouse, opening the new message.

Astrid,

Today you will go to the mall. In your purse I want you to carry with you a bag of ice. Inside the bag of ice you will place your largest glass dildo. When you arrive at the mall, you will head to the bathroom; you will remove all of your clothes, place them in your purse and put your jacket back on. You will browse every store in the mall this way. Every store. After you have finished you will find a clothing store, you will pick out several items and ask to try them on. You will take all of your items to the fitting room and you will masturbate with your dildo until you come. You are not allowed to leave the fitting room until you have an orgasm. To prove to me that you have come, you will soak up all of your juices with one of the items of clothing you have picked out. You will then take it to the register and purchase it. You are then free to dress and leave.

If you fail to do this, you will be punished.

Master Markus

Astrid gasped. Her Master must have been feeling particularly inspired this morning. She imagined him typing out those words, his penis erect as he dreamed up each piece of this challenge for her. He knew how nervous public sex and nudity made her, he knew how hard this would be for her to complete. Maybe he had designed this with the intention of her failing, so he could impose some severe new penalty on her. Master Markus had a system—the harder the challenge he set forth, the larger the punishment for failure—but he was also very generous with his praise and rewards when she did follow his instructions to the letter.

Her hand wandered down to her swollen clit as she read and reread his message. She rubbed slowly, trying to work up the courage to carry out her Master's orders. Her pussy began to ache as she brought herself closer to orgasm; she felt the delicious tension welling up inside her, just waiting for her to push herself over the edge. She pulled her hand away, letting all the wonderful feelings wash away. She was going to wait and come the way her Master wanted her to come.

She jumped out of her chair and began to gather the items requested of her. From her dresser drawer she pulled out a long crystal dildo. It was surprisingly weighty; she held it out in the palm of her hand, testing it. She ran her fingers over its ridges; the texture excited her and she was anxious to feel it inside of her, filling her up.

Next she ran to the kitchen, pulling a large plastic lunch bag from a box, filling it full of ice, sealing her dildo inside as instructed. She was trembling; the butterflies in her stomach had all migrated south and were now fluttering deep inside her pussy.

Dressed and packed, Astrid drove to the mall. This being a Saturday, the mall was packed; she had a hard time finding a place to park. As she circled the lot looking for a spot she had time to think—and thinking made her nervous. She couldn't help but imagine all the people inside, shopping, loitering in the food court and using the dressing rooms. A lump formed in her throat; it wasn't too late for her to just turn around and go home. Master's punishment couldn't be that bad, could it? She stifled a laugh; she knew how absurd that sounded. Besides, she had just found a parking spot, so chickening out wasn't really an option anymore.

Once inside the mall, Astrid headed to the nearest bath-room, her knees weak. She found an empty stall, went inside and closed the door quietly, trying not to draw any attention to herself. She hung her jacket from the hook on the door and began to undress. She folded everything neatly, tucking each item carefully into her bag, making sure not to lose any of its other contents. She shivered, feeling exposed under the clinical fluorescent lighting of the public restroom. She was starting to feel as though her surroundings were beginning to judge her for what she was doing. Astrid quickly reached for her jacket, slipped it on and buttoned it shut. She looked down at her bare legs and silently cursed herself for not owning anything longer; her jacket barely came down to her knees. Even with the jacket on, she still felt totally naked.

Astrid walked sheepishly through the mall, popping into every store, spending a minute or two browsing before moving on to the next. Wet drops of excitement slid down her inner thigh, leaving a slick trail behind. There was nothing she could do about it; if she tried to reach down to wipe it away, she risked drawing attention to herself. When she finally reached the last shop she sighed in relief; she had survived the first challenge and no one was wise to her naughty little secret. She smiled triumphantly. Gripping her purse tight, she steeled herself for round two. She only had to walk a short distance before she spotted a women's clothing store. From the mannequins in the window, it looked like they sold clothes to teen girls and older women who were desperately trying to cling to their twenties. Astrid wrinkled her nose; the stuff on display really wasn't her style, but the clothes didn't really matter—all she needed was the dressing room.

She stepped inside. Astrid looked around to see if anyone had watched her enter. She was starting to feel like a top secret agent on a covert mission for the president, only instead of saving the world, her job was to have a mind-blowing orgasm. Satisfied that no one could care less about her presence, she started browsing the racks, trying to look normal and praying that no shoppers or staff could tell what she was up to.

"Can I help you find something?" a saleswoman asked.

Astrid jumped. "What?" Her eyes went wide, her heart raced.

"Did you need help finding anything?" The saleswoman smiled pleasantly. Astrid was sure she could see the shame written all over her face and dropped her eyes to the floor.

"Just browsing. Thanks," she managed to squeak out, blushing.

"Well, if you need anything, just give me a shout. My name's Natalie."

Astrid nodded, pretending to absorb herself in the contents of the nearest rack. She breathed a sigh of relief when Natalie finally walked away, leaving her free to continue with her mission. Astrid began pulling out clothes, whatever she could reach. She grabbed a black top, a gray tank top, a blue party dress and a pair of shorts she knew was several sizes too small for her. Bounty in hand, Astrid approached the saleswoman. "I'd like to try these on," she mumbled.

"I'm sorry, what was that?" The polite smile remained plastered on Natalie's face.

Astrid held up her pile of clothes. "Could I try these on?" The words caught in her throat and her mouth went dry.

"Do you need a fitting room?" asked Natalie.

Astrid nodded.

"Follow me." Natalie seized the handful of items away from Astrid and sashayed to the back of the store and down a short hallway. Three dressing room stalls lined the far wall at the end of the hall. Astrid swallowed hard; she hadn't realized it would be this small.

"Can I get your name?"

"Astrid."

"That's a different sort of name, isn't it?" Natalie commented as she neatly wrote Astrid's name on a heart-shaped whiteboard that dangled from the door. "Here you go, you're all set." Natalie set the clothes inside the middle dressing room and waved Astrid on in. "I will check on you in a bit."

"No hurry." Astrid tried to smile nonchalantly as she stepped into the room, closing the door behind her.

She leaned against the back of the door for a moment, trying to catch her breath. This was crazy and exhilarating all at the same time, and she didn't know how to process all the things she was feeling. She set her bag down on the bench and unbuttoned her jacket slowly, savoring the way she looked in the full-length mirror. Her face was flushed red, her lips were full and her eyes sparkled with something mischievous. She reached the last button and shrugged out of her jacket, letting it slip to the floor, pooling around her feet. Except for a pair of red heels, her Master's favorite, she was completely naked.

She grinned at her reflection, feeling liberated. She let a hand caress her body, moving along her goose-pimpled flesh. Even her skin was excited. Relaxing, she felt her fears begin to melt and give way to lust. She wanted herself.

Astrid reached down for her bag and opened it. She fished out the bag of ice. It had nearly all melted, her glass dildo floating in the bag of water like an absurd fish won at a carnival. Carefully, she opened the bag and pulled her dildo out. It was cold; the ice had turned the glass toy into an icicle. She dropped her bag to the floor, lowered herself onto the bench and spread her legs wide. She examined her pussy in the mirror. She was pink and swollen; the hood of her clit was pulled back, exposing her hard bud. As Astrid held the dildo a fraction of an inch from her body, the chill sent shivers up her spine. She was sure she could see it fogging up, like breath against a cold windowpane.

She started to work the dildo against her clit, pressing it down into the nub, angling the pressure this way and that, experimenting with what felt good. Astrid sighed, sinking deeper into pleasure. She pulled the dildo down from her clit, resting it against the mouth of her pussy, rolling it around, letting her own juices lubricate the chilled toy. She looked down at the dildo, liking the way the crystal-clear glass gave off a pink glow while pressed against her pussy lips.

"Everything all right in there?" she heard Natalie's voice call from the other side of the door.

Astrid scrambled to reply. "Yes, everything is great, thank you," she barked out hoarsely. She cleared her throat. "It's just really hard to decide which one I like. I might have to try them all on again."

"Okay, take your time." Natalie sounded pleasant but exasperated.

"Oh, I will," Astrid called back, sending the frigid dildo plunging into the depths of her pussy. She let out a deep sigh of satisfaction. The dildo sent cooling waves throughout her body. She couldn't believe how amazing it felt. She pulled the toy out, letting it slide its full length out of her before sending it sailing back in. She closed her eyes, letting herself get lost to pure bliss. She rotated the dildo, sending the hard ridges bumping and grinding against the tender walls of her vagina. She dropped her head and arched her back, imagining her Master between her thighs, his tongue licking every inch of her pussy.

From her bag, her phone chimed. Astrid wanted to ignore it, but what if it was something important? She leaned over and fished the phone from its pocket. It was a text message from her Master.

Are you at the mall?

Yes, she typed back.

A moment later the phone chimed again. *Good girl. There has been a change of plans. I have been thinking about you all morning, I want to hear you come.*

Astrid looked puzzled. *How?*

Call me. Let me listen as you pleasure yourself.

Yes, Sir, she sent back. He wanted her to make noise? He wanted her to make those kinds of noises in here? The dressing room was so small; she could hear someone trying on clothes just to her left. She began to panic. This was too much; she couldn't, she just couldn't do it. She set her phone down, catching a glimpse of herself in the mirror, the long glass dildo still stuffed inside her glistening pussy, her full lips wrapped around the shaft, swallowing it.

As she stared at herself, Astrid felt the familiar ache of desire flow through her. Maybe she could do this. She wanted to please her Master, and more importantly, she wanted to please herself. She took hold of the chilled dildo and began pumping it inside her. With each stroke, the bulbous head pressed against the fleshy ridge of her G-spot. Her phone chimed once more.

Well?

Astride reached down and dialed his number. The call was answered. On the other end all she could hear was Master's familiar voice saying, "Continue." Then the line went silent.

Astrid put a finger on her clit, while her other hand continued to work the dildo in her pussy. She moaned, though the noise was barely audible; she was still nervous that someone would hear. She pushed the dildo in deeper, letting the length of it disappear inside her while she gasped and moaned again. Feeling braver, she began to pick up speed, one hand plunging the glass toy in and out while her other hand left her clit and found its way to her erect nipple. She pinched it between her thumb and fore-finger, rolling it around, pulling it. Another long guttural moan escaped her lips. As she crept closer to orgasm Astrid didn't care who could hear her. This was between her and her Master; the world no longer concerned her.

The toy was now slick as it worked its way around her vagina.

The chill had worn off, leading to a whole new sensation. The hotter she got, the warmer the toy got. She angled the round head up, pushing up into her G-spot. She was ready to let go.

She remembered her Master's last order, the proof he wanted from her. She grabbed the black top and wadded it up under her dripping pussy. It didn't take long before she was able to tip herself past the breaking point. She groaned, biting back a full-blown scream. Her thighs began to quake, her pelvic muscles contracted and beautiful warm liquid squirted out of her pussy. She watched this grand show in the mirror, the waterfall of sex cascading from her quivering hole, flowing down onto the black fabric beneath her, pooling in a milky-white puddle. She leaned back against the wall, slumped in exhaustion, trying to catch her breath.

She remembered the phone beside her. "Hello?" she said, picking up the phone.

"You have done well. But I still need to see proof."

"Oh yes, I have it for you, Sir. I think you will be pleased." Astrid giggled, looking down at the wet shirt.

Master Markus hung up the phone. Astrid threw her toy back into her purse along with her phone. Slipping back into her jacket, she gathered up her clothes and strode confidently to the register.

"Find something that worked for you?" Natalie asked.

"I sure did." Astrid handed over the black top. "I'll take this one." She presented her bank card, smiling. She couldn't wait to take it home and model it for her Master. Maybe he would plan another shopping trip soon.

MUST LOVE DOLLS

Giselle Renarde

It's not like she'd *caught* him browsing for Japanese love dolls. Honor wasn't the kind of wife who checked her husband's Internet history. They didn't hide things from each other. Tom didn't have to disclose what he was shopping for, or awkwardly broach the subject, because his computer was right there on his lap while they watched TV. He simply turned the screen in Honor's direction and asked, "What do you think of Natsuki?"

"Very sexy," Honor said, though her focus remained with *CSI: Miami*.

"Her breasts are huge for an Asian girl, but I guess that's the fantasy."

"Mmm-hmm." Honor glanced at the photo again, trying to piece together what she was seeing: a gorgeous girl in a lime-green fishnet top, big breasts, no bra. Jean cutoffs, shaved pussy, no panties. She looked closer, not at the photo this time, but at the website itself. "Wait, Tom, is she...she's not *real*, is she?"

He laughed. "Real as in flesh and blood? No. No, she's a doll."

Screw *CSI* in all its incarnations—Tom's find was much more interesting.

"She looks almost human, doesn't she?" he asked.

Honor licked her lips as she stared at those perky peach nipples. "More than human. She looks...she looks good enough to eat."

Tom's hand found her thigh. "You want to eat Natsuki, do you?"

"Is she, like, physically...physiologically...?" Honor couldn't remember the word.

"Anatomically?"

"Anatomically, yeah." She took a deep breath, but her lungs quivered. "Is she anatomically correct?"

Honor looked up from the computer screen to meet her husband's self-assured grin. He said, "Natsuki's got it all."

When she arrived at their door, it was like Christmas morning. Natsuki had started life on the other side of the planet, shipped all the way from Australia. She cost nearly as much as Honor's used Honda Civic, but unlike the Civic, Natsuki had no previous owners. Nobody had ever taken this girl for a ride. She and Tom would be the first.

"I haven't stopped thinking about her," Honor said as she scooped handfuls of packing peanuts out of the huge reinforced cardboard box. "Maybe it's the eyes, or the lips. I don't know, but I literally haven't gone one day without fantasizing about this girl since that night you first showed me her picture."

Tom smiled. "I can't remember the last time I saw you so excited about something."

"I get excited about you," she said.

"Yeah, well..." Tom stopped short when he found the bare, soft curve of Natsuki's ass.

They stared in silence, both of them, before scooping those damn peanuts onto the floor like they were bailing out a sinking ship. She was upside down in the box, her fingers and feet mummified with cling film. Her head was bare. The black human-hair wig they'd ordered rested beside her left arm, and Honor picked it up while her husband lifted Natsuki's naked body into his arms. He looked like a firefighter carrying an unconscious woman from a burning building.

"Should we put on the lingerie?" Honor picked that out of the box too. The fishnet stockings, bra, panties and sexy school-girl outfit all came free with purchase.

"I have to put her down," Tom said, struggling. "Man, is she heavy."

He took her upstairs and Honor followed him into the bedroom. She put on the wig right away, because Natsuki looked odd without it. Once her hair was on, her humanity sprang to the fore and Honor felt like…well, it was hard to explain. Her heart raced and her pussy pulsed. She felt hot all over. Maybe this was love.

"Do you know how many nights I've dreamed of what her pussy might look like?"

Tom unwrapped the plastic from Natsuki's hands and feet. "Of course you're going to dream about her pussy—it's the one part they won't show you on their website."

"I wonder why," Honor said.

"To maintain a little mystery, maybe? So you'll buy a ten-thousand-dollar doll just to peek between her legs?"

"More than just peek." Staring at the soft valley of Natsuki's thighs, Honor bit her lip. If she dove right in, what would Natsuki think?

Nothing! She wouldn't think anything. She was a doll, nothing more.

"Did you grab the hairbrush from the box?" Tom was all business. "That wig needs a little tenderness."

Yes, there had been a hairbrush in the box, but no, Honor hadn't picked it up. "I'll use mine."

Tom sat at the foot of the bed, pressing Natsuki's toes, one by one, between his thumb and forefinger. Honor watched him, and she felt as though Natsuki were watching him too, as she brushed the doll's silky black hair. The wig was probably supposed to be secured to the head somehow, but it was a tight enough fit, and who could concentrate on an instruction manual at a time like this?

Honor set the brush on the nightstand and slowly slid her hand down Natsuki's soft shoulder and along her arm.

"You can touch her breasts," Tom said, like he could read Honor's mind. "She's ours now, babe. You can touch wherever you like."

Honor's stomach knotted with nerves as she cupped one of Natsuki's perky silicone breasts. She could hardly breathe as she carried that significant weight on her palm. It had been ages since she'd touched any breast but her own.

"How does it feel?" Tom asked.

"Heavy." She sank onto the bed, wrapping her arms around the love doll, pressing both big breasts together and wishing she were naked too. "Her skin's so soft. Her hair smells like lilies. God, I've missed this."

"Playing with dolls?" Tom asked.

"Playing with women."

He smiled. "I know, babe. Take off your top."

She did him one better and stripped bare. "I'm nothing to look at, compared with Natsuki."

Tom raised an eyebrow. "I'm looking at you."

He always knew the perfect thing to say, and it made her

horny as hell. She grabbed his belt and unbuckled it, then tore into his pants and found his erection. He was as hard as she was wet.

"I want to look between her legs," she told him.

"Who's stopping you?"

When she didn't let go of his cock, he kissed her with a passion so full she could taste it on her tongue. She stroked his shaft, savoring the hardness in her hand. He lifted off his shirt and kicked out of his pants. It wasn't until they were both fully naked that Honor felt the frisson of a voyeuristic stare. She turned to Natsuki, slowing her pace without releasing her husband's erection.

"I wish she could see us," Honor said. "Don't you?"

Tom took a breath before responding. "I kind of feel like...I mean, I know she can't, but..."

"No, I know."

They watched the motionless doll propped up on their pillows, in an almost-seated position. You get what you pay for, and they'd gotten one quality toy.

Pulling her husband closer to the bed, Honor reached for Natsuki's outstretched hand. She half-expected the doll to spring to life when touched, but that didn't happen. Tom sprang to life, though. When Honor wrapped the doll's fingers around his cock, it jumped against her silicone wrist.

"How does that feel, huh?" Honor wrapped her hand around the doll's and forced a stronger grip around his shaft. She and Natsuki jerked him off together. "Good?"

Tom groaned. "You have no idea."

Natsuki's fingers felt almost real inside Honor's fist, and she didn't really want to let go, but she couldn't wait any longer. "I want to see her pussy."

"Me too." Tom took over, wrapping his hand around

Natsuki's slim fingers. "Look at her face, hon. She wants you between her legs."

She did. It was crazy to think so, but Natsuki seemed genuinely enthused about showing off her pussy.

"Crawl up there," Tom said. "Push her legs apart. Get between them."

Their bed had never seemed such a foreign place as when Honor separated the doll's resistant thighs. Her mound was bare, just like in the picture. They'd specified when they ordered that they wanted a slick, clean cunt. Honor kept an impressive bush, but she and Tom both liked the shaved look on other girls.

"Open her up," Tom said. "Look inside."

Honor's hands trembled as she pressed her thumbs to the doll's outer lips and spread them wide. Natsuki's labia looked so sweet and pink and beautiful that a gush of saliva built up under Honor's tongue. The doll's pussy looked about as real as a doll's could possibly look, and the sight took Honor's breath away.

"Would you get a load of that," Tom said as Natsuki continued her hand job. "Was it worth the wait, babe?"

Honor didn't answer his question. Instead, she dove between Natsuki's thighs, pressing her tongue to the love doll's firm little lips. She licked Natsuki's pussy like it was the real thing, tricking her mind into believing that could be true. She touched everywhere, from the doll's smooth thighs to its big, bouncy breasts. When Honor toyed with the nipples, she could have sworn she felt Natsuki flinch.

"You really love a hot, wet pussy, don't you, babe?" Tom opened the cinnamon-flavored lube and squirted some onto Natsuki's bare mound. "Try that out, huh?"

Honor moved the lube with her hands and her lips, sliding the tingling warmth past the doll's little clit and down its realistic folds. Her mouth felt as hot and engorged as her cunt, thanks to the lube. Also thanks to the lube, she could fit her fingers inside Natsuki's sweet pussy. Ohh, that kitty had claws. It sucked her in like a vacuum, clamping down on her two digits, then three digits, like it had muscles and free will.

"How does she feel down there?" Tom's voice betrayed more than just a hint of jealousy as she fucked their doll with her hand.

"So good," Honor said without removing her mouth from Natsuki's cunt. "So hot and wet and tight."

She gasped when Natsuki arched forward, placing her tender little hands on Honor's ass. With Tom's help, Natsuki spread her cheeks. Those fingers felt miraculously real, and as Natsuki's belly pressed up against Honor's head, she turned to find her husband climbing into bed behind her.

"I gotta fuck some pussy," he said. "I don't care if it's hers or yours, but I need that hot hug soon or I'm gonna lose my mind."

"Take me," Honor said, greedy for a fuck. "Take me hard."

Tom's hands pressed against Natsuki's, branding Honor's ass with firm fingers. His cock didn't mess around. It plunged inside Honor's cunt, splashing pussy juice all down her thighs. The sloppy squelch of his thrusts just barely surpassed the wet lap of Honor's tongue on Natsuki's clit.

"If she could talk, what would she say?" Honor asked, before sucking Natsuki's silicone flesh.

"She'd say, 'Don't stop licking my pretty pink puss, you gorgeous girl.'"

Honor's heart fluttered, and so did her pussy. Tom must have felt it, because he moaned and pummeled her harder. The doll bounced with them on the bed as Honor cupped her cool ass, tearing into Natsuki's cunt like a tiger. Her heart raced. Her pussy throbbed.

"I think you're wrong," she said, panting, her chin dripping with saliva and cinnamon lube. "I think she'd say, 'I want that big strong man pounding my slit. I want him inside me.'"

"You think?"

Honor rolled to the side, letting her husband's big cock slip from between her slick lips. She missed his girth already, but she buried that feeling, along with herself, under Natsuki's weighted mass.

Tom's erection bobbed when he laughed. "What the heck are you doing?"

She let Natsuki's beautiful body sink into hers, setting her head to one side of the doll's so their soft cheeks touched. From underneath, Honor wrapped her legs around Natsuki's, spreading them wide for her husband. "Look at that pretty pussy, Tom. It's calling out to be fucked. It wants your cock so bad it's burning up inside."

"You're crazy," he said with a lusty laugh.

"If I'm crazy, so are you."

"Well, that's settled, then." Tom held his cock by the base while Honor cupped Natsuki's heavy tits, juggling them in her hands. "We're both off-the-rocker looney toons."

"Yup." Honor spread Natsuki's lovely legs even wider. "Now fuck this pretty little virgin-whore. She's come all the way from Australia just to see you."

Honor couldn't wait to see the look on her husband's face when he planted his dick in the doll. She spread her fingers so that, when he came down on them, he'd feel Natsuki's hard nipples pressing into his chest. She pushed those tits together as the doll's back compressed her own. Tom watched her as she watched him, and for a moment they were both completely still.

Then, with a growl, he set one hand on Natsuki's shoulder, driving it down against Honor's. With the other hand, he guided his erection to the apex of their virgin's young thighs. He paused there, again, glancing from the doll's face to Honor's. "I can't believe we're really doing this."

"I can." Honor arched until she could see past the doll's breasts and down its flat tummy. "Now go on and stick your prick in her. I'm watching, honey."

His eyes gleamed as he looked from Natsuki's bare pussy to Honor's smiling face, and then back to the pussy. Leaning into the doll, he let out a groan the likes of which Honor hadn't heard since they were first married.

"How's her pussy feel, baby?"

"Oh god, so tight!" He forced himself inside, driving Natsuki's ass against Honor's throbbing mound. "Fuck, that's good."

"Harder, baby."

He laughed, wheezing. "No, I'll come if I go too fast. She's just so...oh..."

His body closed in on hers, sandwiching the love doll between them. As he fucked Natsuki, slow but sure, that smooth silicone rear massaged Honor's cunt. Her heard raced when her husband's lips met hers. Their tongues collided, lashed, smashed, wrapped together caduceus-style. Poor Natsuki was out in the cold—though, not really, considering Tom was ramming her with his cock.

Honor wrapped her legs around her husband's, inadvertently bringing Natsuki's along for the ride. That must have tightened up the doll's pussy, because Tom gasped in her mouth. Their kisses raged.

"Yes," she said without stopping the kiss. "Yes, faster, faster..."

He fucked the doll good and hard, slamming Natsuki's backside into Honor's front. Her clit was so swollen and sensitive that every time the silicone ass touched it she shrieked. This was just too much. Her legs began to shake, entwined as they were with her husband's and their doll's. Below her waist was a raging fire, wet heat that couldn't be extinguished. She rocked her hips, driving Natsuki up toward her husband, almost like they were all one being.

Honor felt everything, every move. And when Tom shrieked and arched, she could have sworn she felt his cock in her cunt. He exploded with come, so much it dripped out of Natsuki's pussy and down hers. She hugged the doll hard.

They stayed in that configuration until the collective weight of a husband and a love doll grew too much to bear. Tom rolled off and they set Natsuki between them in the bed, both tracing their hands across her soft, smooth skin. Every time their fingers met in the middle, a spark passed between them and Honor smiled. Even after she'd closed her eyes, she could tell that Tom was smiling too.

After a long, dozy while, Tom said, "We should probably get dinner started, huh?"

Honor turned to look at the bedside clock. "Jeez, yeah. No wonder I'm so hungry."

They didn't move, except to finger Natsuki's sopping pussy or squeeze her peachy tits. This body was always ready and, god, was it ever hot.

Tom's stomach gurgled and the doll's spell was broken. "Okay, for real this time." He hobbled out of bed and stretched his arms up in the air, then found some clothes to put on.

Honor took a little longer to roll out of bed. By the time she'd pulled on a pair of pajama pants and a T-shirt, Tom was downstairs rattling pans. She pulled the sheets up over Natsuki's breasts so the doll wouldn't get cold, and it took a few seconds to register how crazy that would sound if she said it out loud.

Natsuki looked restful, despite her open eyes. She relaxed in the middle of the bed, sprawling halfway onto Tom's side, halfway onto Honor's. Her hair had been delightfully tussled. They'd have to clean her pussy out before they fucked her again, but that could wait until after dinner. Honor's stomach burbled too, and she turned toward the door.

But before she left the bedroom, she pressed her finger down on the bedside clock, turning on the radio. Adult Contemporary was generally a crowd-pleaser, but even if Natsuki didn't like the music, at least she'd have some form of company. Honor didn't want their doll getting lonely while she and her husband were out of the room.

SEX SELLS

Adriana Ravenlust

Y ou know society has gone to shit when companies start popping up with orgasm insurance. No, really. I know how crazy it sounds, and I'm the door-to-door insurance salesman. Woman? Whatever.

It all started in 2013. That's when they began experimenting with electrical impulses to the brain. The idea was to stimulate neural pathways. You'd be able to recall information better in the future. Some people were hopeful that this would lead to a cure for Alzheimer's—and it did—but that's not what the science eventually became used for. One day, while researchers were experimenting with stimulating specific parts of the brain, their human subject orgasmed.

Oh, I'm sure it was as awkward as could be. I bet the scientists wrote it off the first few times. But then it kept happening. Again and again. Science had finally discovered what men never could: how to guarantee a partner's orgasm. Finally, one bold researcher decided to see how electrical stimulation of the brain could really help enable orgasms.

At first, they considered only the ramifications for married couples. Science is rather conservative, after all. But they didn't stop there. Eventually, scientists were able to give just about anyone an orgasm by plugging electrodes into the patient's skull—trust me, they use a lot more finesse nowadays—and letting off an electrical charge.

It wasn't enough that some people were finally able to achieve orgasm and explore their sexual sides. Once the sex toy industry got wind of the idea, things really took on a life of their own. Researchers began to look at how they could make orgasms even better and allow users to control devices to give their partners orgasms on demand. Cybersex was forever changed, and sex toy manufacturers raced to be the first to incorporate this technology into their toys.

That brings us to today. Right now. The COME industry— that's Controlled Orgasm via Measured Electricity for those of you not in the know—is well established. Of course, it went through a rough patch those first few years. Researchers had to prove there weren't any lasting side effects and that home users could safely use the technology. In the end, the sex toy makers had to go through a labyrinthine approval process to get their products on the market. But they did it, and the shelves of sex toy stores and even Walgreens are now fully stocked with COME toys.

The most common method involves a small adhesive electrode that you place at the nape of your neck. The electrode connects to a control pack—yes, we call it the COME-troller— that allows it to emit the precise type of electricity required to cause orgasm. To be honest, I don't know the science of it. You see, I've never even used it.

I'm kind of the odd duck out when it comes to COME toys, no pun intended. They just never interested me. So how did I get into selling orgasm insurance for it? Well, it's a long story, but I'll sum it up.

The research wasn't quite as honest as consumers would have believed, but by the time the first users realized that COME was eventually making it difficult or even impossible to, well, come anymore, sex toy manufacturers had the government in their pocket. It was like oil companies in the twentieth century—but worse. The toys stayed on the market, and the manufacturers were able to keep the bad news out of the media for a while by settling lawsuits quietly.

However, this couldn't last forever. More reports began popping up. The companies had to respond. Eventually, someone had a great idea: let's insure the user's orgasm. We'll give them a nice payout if their COME toys inhibit their ability to orgasm and everyone will be happy. Now, you would think consumers might be smarter about this, that they would realize the people behind this were the very same sex toy retailers who were selling them products that interfered with their ability to have orgasms.

You would be wrong.

Consumers were hooked, maybe even addicted. And politicians were getting rich. Orgasm insurance was a go.

This is how it works. Buyers opt into an insurance plan when they buy their COME toy. They can choose the premium they pay. The more frequently they use their toy, the higher their premium tends to be. This comes with a higher payout should the technology make it impossible to orgasm in the future. It's nothing groundbreaking. In fact, the idea is so simple that most people probably passed it off as too ridiculous to work. But it did.

And now I work at selling this insurance. Why? Mostly because I suddenly found myself an out-of-work divorcée. I didn't have many skills after spending ten years enjoying the company of my husband—that is, until he cheated on me. The insurance company wanted saleswomen who were relatively attractive, confident and well spoken. I guess I fit the bill.

My days are not as weird as you might expect, however. I don't actually go door to door. Sometimes I host workshops for sex toy retailers. I field a lot of phone calls about insurance when I'm in the office, and sometimes the company sends me to someone's home for a personalized presentation. Those some-ones are well-to-do, and I charm them as well as I know how.

This was one of those days. Except it was a little out of the ordinary. The couple I would be visiting—he was some sort of broker and she was a kept woman half his age—hadn't yet purchased a COME toy. My boss had instructed me that I was attempting to sell both the toy and the insurance. It was strange, yes, but I liked the challenge. When I arrived at their home, I was surprised. It was more modest than the homes of my previous customers, but the couple was still perfectly presented. He answered the door with a practiced smile upon his face and led me to a clean, contemporary sitting room. I took the time to look him over over as I followed him inside. His hair was short and he had a physique that suggested he spent some time at the gym after work. She was perched on a couch, posture correct with her hands folded delicately in her lap. Her hair was darker than his, almost what you'd called raven, and she was as svelte as her husband. She was quiet, letting her husband speak. Was she aloof or just shy? It was difficult to tell.

It was easier to launch into selling the COME toy than I'd expected. I guess I'd become a better salesperson since I started this job. My ex-husband would certainly have been surprised to see my charming smile and persuasive speech then—I could never seem to convince him of anything while we were married.

I went over the specs, glossing over the science and focusing on the safety and effectiveness of the toy. I assured the couple that they certainly knew others who enjoyed COME-ing, as people called it these days. This seemed to make the young wife uncomfortable. She excused herself to "prepare us tea."

The husband, Jonathan, was more eager, however. He launched into a story about his coworker's wife. Apparently, she had been a frigid bitch but her COME toy enabled her to be multiorgasmic and saved the marriage. I wasn't so sure about that, but the story was just one to pass the time. I didn't realize his real angle until I heard him ask his next question.

"So do you like to COME?" There was a twinkle in his eye. He thought it was clever. I had heard my fair share of bad puns about the thing. I had never heard it aimed at myself before, though. I stammered, knowing I'd have to lie. No one likes to buy something that the salesman wouldn't personally use.

"Of course I do." At that moment his wife returned to the room.

"Do what?"

Her voice startled me. It had an edge that was more powerful than her meekly feminine appearance conveyed. It was deep for a woman, delicious to listen to.

"Enjoy the COME machine, miss. I mean, ma'am." I felt as though she had walked in on us, like I had with my husband and his dirty little secret. She wasn't at all upset, however.

"Oh. Perhaps you'd like to show us, then." Her tone made it clear this was a command, not a request. I suddenly reexamined my assessment of this relationship. Perhaps he was the kept one.

"Well, I'm not entirely sure that would be appropriate."

"I'm not entirely sure that I want to purchase something without seeing how it works." There was a challenge in the air as she replied.

"Perhaps you'd like to try it out personally, in your bedroom..." I offered.

"I want to see *you* come." The challenge was verbalized. There was no skirting the issue. I no longer cared about selling the toy. My natural reaction was to accept any challenge issued to me, and my primal instincts caused me to forget about the strange situation I had walked into.

I hadn't noticed the wife—was her name Audrey?—moving toward me. Yet, there she was by my side, the COME toy in her hand.

"So you place the electrode on the back of the neck." She parroted my brief explanation back to me. Her hand wrapped around my neck, fingers pressing the electrode to my skin. I thought I felt a shock run down my spine, but she hadn't even turned it on yet.

"And you can control the device with this button." Another statement, not a question. Her thumb circled the button, but the COME machine was still off. Her hand rested against my neck, her fingers lightly curled against my skin. I didn't know why, but I couldn't take my eyes off her.

"Y-yes. That's how it works." The words fell out of my mouth awkwardly.

"And the person doesn't need to be aroused at all to achieve orgasm?" I shook my head.

"Are you aroused right now?" I wanted to lie. I tried to lie. I ached to lie. But I couldn't.

"Yes, I am." Audrey smiled, the type of smile that makes you forget anyone else exists in the world. I wondered if her husband felt the same way about her as I did in that moment. Her husband! I'd almost forgotten him. I turned my head to look at Jonathan. He was watching us intently, but I couldn't tell if he was enjoying it.

Audrey seized that moment to make her move. She leaned in toward the exposed skin of my neck as I turned, planting soft but hungry kisses along my neck. I gasped, my skin tingling. She motioned for her husband to come closer, handing him the controller to the toy. So he was the kept one, after all.

With the COME-troller in his hands, she was able to use both of hers to stimulate me. Her delicate fingers worked the buttons out of the loops of my blouse. Audrey licked her lips as she noticed the front clasp on my bra. Her lithe fingers unclasped my bra, exposing my breasts. I was especially fond of them. I guess she was, too. She lifted each breast to draw my nipples into her mouth. They were already erect before touching her lips. Yes, I was aroused, and my body couldn't keep it a secret.

But she didn't want to just stand around. Her finger hooked into my plain A-line skirt, which I had never before considered anything but business-appropriate, and she pulled me back toward an oversized armchair, Jonathan in tow. At first, I thought she would have me sit, but Audrey perched on the chair herself and dropped her hands down to the sides of my thighs. She shimmied my skirt up to my waist, revealing simple thigh-high stockings and my hipster panties. I almost wished I'd put on something spectacular that morning—but I'd never taken off my clothes at work before.

Audrey patted either side of the chair behind her, motioning for me to straddle her. I did, Jonathan following close enough behind me that the electrode on the back of my neck stayed in place. I must have looked precariously perched, because he stepped closer behind me, his body bracing mine. The sudden presence startled me, but I leaned my shoulders and head against his abdomen, grateful for the support.

Audrey had been intently examining my body and my wardrobe, but she wasn't one to waste time. Her fingers snaked between my panties and my body, pushing the fabric to the side. Her hands were warm against my vulva, lightly stroking it before parting my lips. I shivered at her touch.

She pushed me farther back against her husband as she tenuously slid a finger into my pussy. I was so ready. She could tell, and she inserted another finger, then another. I was full with this stranger, but somehow it felt perfectly natural to let her pleasure my body.

Audrey wasn't done, however. As her fingers inside me began stroking my G-spot, her thumb caressed my clitoris. She held me tight within her grasp, my pubic bone providing her the handhold to keep me perfectly positioned as she drove me toward orgasm.

It only took a few minutes of her expert fingers and thumb working together for me to feel the familiar tension build in my pussy. Audrey could tell, too.

"You like the way I treat your cunt, don't you?" I was startled by her sudden speech and abrasive language but no less turned on. I nodded. It wasn't enough for her. Audrey slapped her open palm against my breasts.

"Yes, I do." The sudden assault took me by surprise, but Audrey knew exactly what she was doing. The slap was my undoing. I was well on my way to orgasm—and without the assistance of the COME toy at all.

She hadn't forgotten about it, however. With a subtle movement that didn't deter her expert strokes, she raised her gaze to meet Jonathan's eyes. I didn't know who she was talking to when she said, "Come, now," but my body didn't wait any longer to heed her command.

It took her husband a brief second to turn on the machine and hit the button. When the first jolt of electricity tickled my brain, I was already mid-orgasm. But my brain responded anyway, piling wave upon wave atop my natural climax. This explosion was longer and more powerful than any orgasm I'd had in my life. My muscles contracted as my body shook. My orgasm seemed to radiate throughout my body. I was convinced that this couple had as much—if not more—to do with my powerful orgasm than the COME toy.

I would have collapsed were it not for Jonathan bracing my body from behind. He remained perfectly stoic as a near-stranger orgasmed on his wife's lap. I wondered if his eyes glistened the way hers did at causing my orgasm.

An orgasm doesn't last forever, of course. Mine soon died down, and I was left short of breath and covered with a dewy sheen of sweat. Jonathan gently helped me to my feet, smoothing my skirt down and removing the COME electrode from the back of my neck. I licked my lips, suddenly thirsty for the promised tea that had never arrived.

"I guess we'll take one," Jonathan remarked, mostly to break the silence.

"And we'll take the toy with your highest level of insurance, too," Audrey chimed in after her husband.

The shock I felt knowing that Jonathan hadn't been talking about the toy when he said they wanted one must have registered on my face because Audrey laughed, but I knew she wasn't kidding. I wasn't sure that I minded, either. I had just made the biggest sale of my life without even trying. I was sure that my boss would be thrilled with my work, however, just like Jonathan and his wife would be thrilled with their new acquisition.

MY LIFE AS A VIBRATOR

Livia Ellis

I come into existence on a Thursday in a factory in the Guang-dong province. My first sensation is of touch. The firm yet well-seasoned hands of my maker, Hui Zhong, have smoothed and stroked my pearlescent pink silicone shell. Although I will never know, I can guess from the brief time we spend together that she is a woman who takes immense care with everything she turns her attention to. I particularly like the brilliant red of the scarf that covers her steel-wool hair. The intense scrutiny of her glaucoma-wrecked eyes misses nothing. I know truly for the first time what it is to live when she slips the pair of C batteries into my innards and gives my bottom a twirl.

I whorl, I jiggle, I shimmy, I shake. I do what Hui Zhong built me to do—I vibrate. For the first time, by doing what I was built to do, I make someone smile. I please her and I please her well.

Unbeknownst to me as she turns me off, then guts me of my batteries, our time together is short-lived. Into a bin with my brothers I go. I wait for her soft hands to hold me again, but it will not happen. No. My first love is found and lost in an instant.

In short order, I am boxed and packed. The next time I see light I am in a warehouse. My home becomes a metal shelf where I rest between boxes of electric kettles and cartons of squeeze bottles of PVA glue.

It is a strange existence. One by one my shelf mates are taken to a fate and a destination unknown. All we can do in our boxes tantalizingly marked SLICK BULLET WATERPROOF SILICONE POWER PENIS is wait and speculate.

The very moment I give up on ever leaving my shelf and discovering what rests beyond aisle 36, section 44, a hand reaches out and picks me. Together with a book on Spanish cookery, a garlic press, *Pride and Prejudice* and a box of high-lighter pens, I am packed in a box and shipped.

My journey is nothing short of excruciating. Between the superiority of *Pride and Prejudice* and the insufferable effervescence of the highlighter pens, I nearly lose what sanity I have left.

At last, joy of joys, I arrive at my destination. The light coming into the box after so long in the dark is like a rainbow after the flood.

A blonde woman examines me, then dismisses me. I want to see the love in her eyes I saw in Hui Zhong's dark pools. There is no love, simply satisfaction. I am nothing more or less than what she expected. I'm crushed.

Hope returns along with her. She holds a length of crimson and gold paper. I'm rolled, tumbled and wrapped. I am a gift. All I can do once again is wait.

I'm transported again. The red curtain of paper conceals a number of laughing women. Anticipation of what might come charges me.

With a shock of surprise, the paper is ripped away from me. At last my surroundings are revealed. I'm held within my box between the hands of a blue-eyed brunette wearing a sparkling tiara. A princess. No, a queen!

A banner on the wall proclaims HAPPY BIRTHDAY DINA!

My queen. My Dina.

Her laughter as she gazes at me is loud and animalistic. The look in her eyes promises passion to come. She's a tigress, my Dina.

With long fingernails, she slices my box open. I'm taken from my packaging and held up proudly for all to see. The ladies cry and laugh as Dina displays me. I don't know where the batteries come from, but I know when I'm opened and they're inserted. With a twist of my base I come to life for the second time.

For all my worth, I put on the best show I can. The women are delighted. Dina switches me off too soon. She sets me to the side, but I know I'll be back in her hands soon enough.

After gifts there is cake and wine. Wine seems to be the focus of the evening, which is probably why no one notices when a hand grasps me, then quickly conceals me in the flouncy folds of a silk skirt.

Together we slip into the bathroom. It is my Dina. She turns on the faucet. My pink silicone shell is baptized under the stream of warm water. The water is left running.

Her foot kicks up and lands on the edge of the sink. The edge of her skirt is slid up, up, up to her waist.

Naughty Dina, who's not wearing any panties, reveals her pretty pink pussy.

When she stretches her leg and moves her bottom, her vagina opens like a blooming flower. Do I dare be so cliché as to think of her pink petals as a flower? How can I not be? They make a flower. A pretty flower I want to explore.

Two fingers probe and explore her sex. I envy those fingers but only for a moment. I'm not neglected for long.

With a twist to my bottom, I come to life.

My slippery and slightly wet, shimmering-pink tip draws a line around the bulge of her clit to the entrance. Slippery with want, I easily slide inside of her. Those thighs squeeze together around me, then release.

I curse a knock on the door.

"Occupied," Dina calls out.

With a flick of her wrist I'm turned off.

"It's me." I know this voice. It is the voice of she who procured me.

"I'll be out in a minute," Dina responds.

I rest silently and nervously in her hot body.

"Just open the door."

Dina snorts indelicately. Her leg comes down from the counter, but I remain in place. The door opens. The door closes. The lock is again engaged.

"What are you doing in here?" There is concern in the woman's voice. She needn't worry. My Dina has me to answer to her needs. I will care for her.

"I'm testing my new vibrator."

There is a pause.

"Seriously?"

"Yes. Does everyone know I'm in here? Are they looking for me? I'm not walking out there with a vibrator in my hand. Go get my purse."

"Nobody noticed you went to the bathroom. They're all drunk. Wanda turned on porn. They're all laughing like they've never seen porn. I came looking for you because we're ordering pizza and I wanted to know what you wanted. Are you really testing your new vibrator?"

"I really am."

"And?"

She wriggles around me. "Nice."

"Show me."

Dina laughs with spirit. This request makes her nervous, but it also heats up her core. This woman is bold and she likes it. Her foot returns to the counter. Her skirt is edged up to her waist. I feel lighter as my base is revealed.

"Going with the natural look?"

I resent this judgment. I like her hairy pussy. The way the hair rubs against me is an explosion of sensation.

The skirt covers me. "Fuck off."

"I'm teasing you. Do you remember when we were in college?"

"I remember."

"Do you remember when we were single and bored and kind of drunk, what we would do?"

"I remember."

"Want to do that?"

Dina doesn't answer. The skirt rises up. I'm reactivated. Dina sighs.

At first I'm twisted in slow circles. Then I slide in and out. Gentle and slow. The sudden feel of a sweet-tipped tongue tapping against me as it slides around Dina's clit revs my vibration.

Between me and the tongue, we generate an orgasm that begins as a flicker deep within Dina's core. There is a tremble inside of her that matches the low intensity of my vibration. Gradually, a wave increases in strength as it reaches for the shore. Her body shudders and her muscles clench around me as an orgasm shakes us to the core.

I'm turned off and taken from her too soon. I could rest

forever insider her luscious hot body. The woman sets me on the counter.

"Do you want to hook up tonight?" the woman asks my Dina.

A thousand times yes, I silently urge Dina. Let me prove I'm a worthy gift.

"Yes."

Oh sweet Dina! Yes, oh yes!

What happens next is a mystery. I'm slid inside the woman's trousers. The door is opened. The next thing I know I'm being placed in a dark room where all I can do is wait and wonder what will happen next.

The answer to all of my questions comes after just enough of a wait for the anticipation to make the revelation pleasure itself.

A lamp gently illuminates the room. My Dina and her friend waste no time removing their clothing.

I can watch from my vantage point on the nightstand, but I'm not invited to participate in what happens next.

The woman—I learn her name is Eva during their exchange—is long and lean. My Dina is petite and beautifully busty.

They come together on the bed. Nipples are plucked and pulled. Lips are pressed together as tongues wrestle in eager mouths.

What I earlier assumed was a criticism of Dina's lush pelt of a pussy was in fact a compliment. As Eva rubs her bare mound against Dina's silky hair, she purrs and moans. Clearly I'm not the only one that's a fan of the sensation. They tumble together as their legs scissor through the sheets.

A hand snakes out of their tumble of limbs to snatch me from my spot on the nightstand. With a sharp shudder I shake into action. The full length of me is thrust into an obscenely slippery pussy that radiates heat. A hairless and trembling pussy. The feel of Eva's slick, silky skin slathered in wetness wrapped around my silicone shaft rivals the tickle of Dina's furry cunt.

In Dina's hand, I penetrate and pleasure Eva. She is alternatively rough then gentle. I'm pulled from her core with a whir of disappointment, quickly exchanged for a rumble of delight.

Naughty, naughty Dina, my precious minx. Just when I think she's done with me, I'm put to greater use. A condom is slipped over my length. A shimmery kimono of latex ribbed and nubbed for her pleasure. Into her own vagina I go. Deep inside her channel, I rapidly and rhythmically tremble as she nimbly loops her leg over Eva's to press their distended clits together. Her body moves in tiny twitches, making those little buttons rub.

I feel the orgasm forming in Dina, possibly before she feels it herself, so deep do I rest within her body. When she senses its building power, she stops. I do not understand this woman. I only wish to pleasure her, but still she resists allowing that moment of ecstasy to overwhelm her.

Then I understand. She edges up Eva's body until her pussy is poised over her mouth. Eva requires no instructions. The tip of her tongue probes Dina's slit. Circles, flutters, swirls and licks. That rough tongue, when it is flat and firm against her slit, looks like it's licking ice cream. Again an orgasm builds. At last my Dina just lets it overcome her. From her toes to her nose, but mostly in her belly, Dina clenches then releases in pure delight.

She falls to her back on the bed. I slip out as her taxed muscles unclench.

Eva leans over her. They kiss. Dina is nudged into movement. Eva's limbs are heavy, yet they respond to Eva's want.

Her hand grips me. The sharp juddering becomes a gentle trembling as my intensity is adjusted. Dina removes the condom and I am sheathed with a new one. We tumble together over Eva, pressing her back into the bed. My tip gently explores the folds of her pussy. The way they touch changes. They're gentler and less frantic. The strokes of their palms are longer and softer. The kisses are deeper. I observe from below as they make love.

Dina encourages Eva to roll onto her stomach and she does. Her round bottom rises over her firm thighs. I understand why Dina enjoys running her hand over those lovely mounds. Slight nudges from Dina's free hand and Eva's knees open akimbo. I'm left to the side as Dina slides into that open space. Her hands squeeze, roll and separate Eva's asscheeks.

She picks me up. Her fingers hold me tight as with the gentlest of probing of my tip, together we find the pucker of Eva's anus. I'm slippery already, but the application of a dab of lubricant makes me all the more slick. I edge into that tight space one gentle nudge at a time until I'm moved no more.

Dina is skilled with her fingers. It is a beautiful torment for Eva to be brought slowly to her own release. Like a Ferris wheel slowly making its ascent to the top, her orgasm rises and rises. She sighs more than screams. It's different from Dina's belly-rattling internal shock, but no less enjoyable.

Gentle fingers remove me from Eva's body. I'm turned off. For a second time I'm washed under a stream of warm water. My first time will hopefully not be my best time.

But if it is, if this is to be my life, my life as a vibrator, then a happy one it will be.

ABOUT THE AUTHORS

VALERIE ALEXANDER lives in Arizona. Her work has been previously published in *Best of Best Women's Erotica, Best Bondage Erotica* and other anthologies.

E. BELLAMY's stories and poems are published or forthcoming in *Ray's Road Review, Poydras Review, Emerge Literary Journal, Umbrella Factory Magazine* and others.

KITTEN BOHEME (kittenboheme.com), besides being an avid reader and writer of erotica, is also a published playwright. When not writing, she pursues her interests in the European aristocracy and the occult. She lives a nomadic lifestyle with Franklin, her cat, and an angry goldfish, Sir Swimsalot.

JILLIAN BOYD (ladylaidbare.com) is the author of numerous erotic short stories and has been published by the likes of Cleis Press, House of Erotica and Constable and Robinson. She lives with her adorable boyfriend in London, where she blogs, bakes and dreams about wild, uninhibited romance while hanging the laundry.

ELIZABETH COLDWELL (elizabethcoldwell.wordpress. com) lives and writes in London. Her stories have appeared in numerous anthologies, including *Best Bondage Erotica 2011, 2012, 2013* and *2014*.

Born in one country, raised in a second and living in a third, **J. CRICHTON** is a teacher and translator who uses her jet-setting experiences as inspiration for steamy writing. She is a firm believer in chasing dreams, happy endings and great sex.

KATHLEEN DELANEY-ADAMS is a stone high femme porn author, word performer and the artistic director of BODY HEAT: Femme Porn Tour. Kathleen's erotic fiction will be featured in several kinky, smutty anthologies set for release in 2014 and 2015, including *She Who Must Be Obeyed* and *The Big Book of Submission: 69 Kinky Tales*.

JOCELYN DEX (JocelynDex.com) writes erotic paranormal and contemporary romance. She loves animals, likes beer and it's rumored she sleeps with a machete beside her bed in case zombies attack in the middle of the night. She believes in hot sex and happily-ever-afters.

LIVIA ELLIS is an American writer living and working in Dublin, Ireland.

ZEE GIOVANNI (sweetjuice.org) is an award-winning writer and professional smutress. With her partner, Damani Starr, she cofounded Sweet Juice Publishing for the erotic liberation of all people, especially kinky people, queer people, trans people, and people of color.

DENA HANKINS (denahankins.net) writes aboard her boat, wherever she has sailed it. After eight years as a sex educator, she started telling erotic tales with far-flung settings—India, North Carolina, deep space—and continued with a queer/trans romance novel, *Blue Water Dreams*, about magnetism and self-sufficiency.

KATYA HARRIS lives in the UK with her family and three crazy rat boys. You can find her on Twitter @Katya_Harris. She hopes you like what she's written, and that you'll come back for more.

OLIVER HOLLANDAIZE is the pseudonym of a frustrated artist who lives and works in San Francisco, CA. He rides his bike to work and owns more than a few sex toys, but has yet to add a Boink Bike to his collection.

MALIN JAMES (malinjames.com) is a writer with a book fetish. Her stories have appeared in numerous anthologies including *Best Women's Erotica 2015*, *Chemical (se)X* and *The Big Book of Orgasms: 69 Sexy Stories*.

CHRIS KOMODO (tinyurl.com/ckomodo) is a California-based artist and writer. He expanded into erotica in 2012 and his work now appears in several erotic anthologies. When he's not working, the thirtysomething Komodo restores furniture and experiments with growing strange varieties of chili peppers. He tweets @SpicyKomodo.

ERRICA LIEKOS (cumisnotaverb.blogspot.com) finally realized she could write whatever filthy things she wanted so long as she used a pseudonym. Don't tell her kids. She was most recently published in Violet Blue's *Best Women's Erotica 2014* anthology.

ADRIANA RAVENLUST turned her nonstop thoughts about sex into a sex toy review and sexuality blog at ofsexandlove.com. Her brand of feminism, geekery and cat-lady craziness has flourished online.

Award-winning erotica writer **GISELLE RENARDE** is a queer Canadian contributor to more than one hundred short-story anthologies and author of juicy books like *Anonymous, Nanny State* and *My Mistress' Thighs*. Ms. Renarde lives across from a park with two bilingual cats who sleep on her head.

ROB ROSEN (therobrosen.net), award-winning author of the novels *Sparkle: The Queerest Book You'll Ever Love, Divas Las Vegas, Hot Lava, Southern Fried, Queerwolf, Vamp* and *Queens of the Apocalypse*, and editor of the anthologies *Lust in Time* and *Men of the Manor*, has had short stories featured in more than 180 anthologies.

SYBIL RUSH (nouveaugrotto.blogspot.com.au) is currently a research scientist and erotica writer. However, she has been—at various times—a striptease artist, a topless dancer, an enlisted soldier and a midwife. Her stories can be found in *Valentine's Day* and *Shameless Behavior.*

CORRINE A. SILVER (Twitter: @CorrineASilver) has been writing stories and fantasies for as long as she can remember, but only recently started trying to get them published. She believes in sex positivity and the incredible allure of enthusiastic consent.

SUSAN ST. AUBIN has been writing erotica for thirty years, sometimes as Jean Casse. Her work appears in *Yellow Silk, Libido, Herotica, Best Lesbian Erotica, Best American Erotica, Best Women's Erotica* and other anthologies. Her story collection, *A Love Drive-By: Stories of Ambition, Hunger, and Desire,* was published in 2011 by Renaissance E Books/Sizzler Editions.

KAMALA ST. DEEDS tells tales of fantasy and science fiction with an erotic twist. She lives in Virginia with her husband, two kids and a curmudgeon of a cat.

ABOUT
THE EDITOR

RACHEL KRAMER BUSSEL (rachelkramerbussel.com) is a New Jersey–based author, editor and blogger. She is the author of *Sex & Cupcakes: A Juicy Collection of Essays* and a sex columnist for *Philadelphia City Paper* and *DAME*. She has edited over fifty books of erotica, including *The Big Book of Submission; The Big Book of Orgasms; Hungry for More; Anything for You: Erotica for Kinky Couples; Baby Got Back: Anal Erotica; Suite Encounters; Going Down; Irresistible; Gotta Have It; Obsessed; Women in Lust; Surrender; Orgasmic; Cheeky Spanking Stories; Bottoms Up; Spanked: Red-Cheeked Erotica; Fast Girls; Do Not Disturb; Tasting Him; Tasting Her; Please, Sir; Please, Ma'am; He's on Top; She's on Top; Caught Looking; Hide and Seek* and is *Best Bondage Erotica* series editor. Her anthologies have won eight IPPY (Independent Publisher) Awards, and *Surrender* won the National Leather Association Samois Anthology Award. Her work has been published in over one hundred anthologies,

including *Best American Erotica 2004* and *2006.* She wrote
the popular "Lusty Lady" column for the *Village Voice.*
Rachel has written for *AVN, Bust,* Cleansheets.com, *Cosmo-
politan, Curve,* The Daily Beast, Elle.com, TheFrisky.com,
Glamour, Harper's Bazaar, Huffington Post, *Inked,* Medi-
abistro, *Newsday, New York Post, New York Observer,*
Penthouse, The Root, Salon, *San Francisco Chronicle,* Time.
com, *Time Out New York* and *Zink,* among others. She has
appeared on *The Gayle King Show, The Martha Stewart Show,*
The Berman and Berman Show, NY1 and Showtime's *Family*
Business. She hosted the popular In the Flesh Erotic Reading
Series, featuring readers from Susie Bright to Zane, and speaks
at conferences, does readings and teaches erotic writing workshops across the country. She blogs at lustylady.blogspot.com
and tweets @raquelita.

More from Rachel Kramer Bussel

Do Not Disturb
Hotel Sex Stories
Edited by Rachel Kramer Bussel

A delicious array of hotel hookups where it seems like anything can happen—and quite often does. "If *Do Not Disturb*
were a hotel, it would be a 5-star hotel with the luxury of
24/7 entertainment available."—Erotica Revealed
978-1-57344-344-9 $14.95

Bottoms Up
Spanking Good Stories
Edited by Rachel Kramer Bussel

As sweet as it is kinky, *Bottoms Up*
will propel you to pick up a paddle
and share in both pleasure and pain,
or perhaps simply turn the other
cheek.
ISBN 978-1-57344-362-3 $15.95

Orgasmic
Erotica for Women
Edited by Rachel Kramer Bussel

What gets you off ? Let *Orgasmic*
count the ways...with 25 stories
focused on female orgasm, there is
something here for every reader.
ISBN 978-1-57344-402-6 $14.95

Surrender
*Erotic Tales of Female Pleasure and
Submission*
Edited by Rachel Kramer Bussel

Bondage, spanking, sex parties, power play
and more—these women go deep into the
heart of submission to experience the thrill
of physical and mental acquiescence.
ISBN 978-1-57344-652-5 $14.95

Women in Lust
Erotic Stories
Edited by Rachel Kramer Bussel

At its best, lust is intense, all-consuming,
leaving you breathless, able only to focus
on slaking that urgent need. The characters
in *Women in Lust* give in to that pure, over-
powering impulse for sex.
ISBN 978-1-57344-724-9 $14.95

Many More than Fifty Shades of Erotica

Please, Sir
Erotic Stories of Female Submission
Edited by Rachel Kramer Bussel

If you liked *Fifty Shades of Grey,* you'll love the explosive stories of *Please, Sir.* These damsels delight in the pleasures of taking risks to be rewarded by the men who know their deepest desires. Find out why nothing is as hot as the power of the words "Please, Sir."
ISBN 978-1-57344-389-0 $14.95

Yes, Sir
Erotic Stories of Female Submission
Edited by Rachel Kramer Bussel

Bound, gagged or spanked—or controlled with just a glance—these lucky women experience the breathtaking thrills of sexual submission. *Yes, Sir* shows that pleasure is best when dispensed by a firm hand.
ISBN 978-1-57344-310-4 $15.95

He's on Top
Erotic Stories of Male Dominance and Female Submission
Edited by Rachel Kramer Bussel

As true tops, the bossy hunks in these stories understand that BDSM is about exulting in power that is freely yielded. These kinky stories celebrate women who know exactly what they want.
ISBN 978-1-57344-270-1 $14.95

Best Bondage Erotica 2014
Edited by Rachel Kramer Bussel

Let *Best Bondage Erotica 2014* be your kinky playbook to erotic restraint—from silk ties and rope to shiny cuffs, blindfolds and so much more. These stories of forbidden desire will captivate, shock and arouse you.
978-1-62778-012-4 $15.95

Luscious
Stories of Anal Eroticism
Edited by Alison Tyler

Discover all the erotic possibilities that exist between the sheets and between the cheeks in this daring collection. "Alison Tyler is an author to rely on for steamy, sexy page turners! Try her!"—Powell's Books
ISBN 978-1-57344-760-7 $15.95

Happy Endings Forever and Ever

Unleash Your Favorite Fantasies

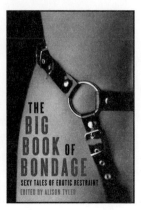

Try This at Home!

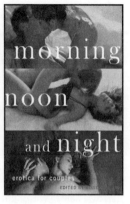

Best Erotica Series

"Gets racier every year."—*San Francisco Bay Guardian*

**Buy 4 books,
Get 1 *FREE****

Best Women's Erotica 2014
Edited by Violet Blue
ISBN 978-1-62778-003-2 $15.95

Best Women's Erotica 2013
Edited by Violet Blue
ISBN 978-1-57344-898-7 $15.95

Best Women's Erotica 2012
Edited by Violet Blue
ISBN 978-1-57344-755-3 $15.95

Best Bondage Erotica 2014
Edited by Rachel Kramer Bussel
ISBN 978-1-62778-012-4 $15.95

Best Bondage Erotica 2013
Edited by Rachel Kramer Bussel
ISBN 978-1-57344-897-0 $15.95

Best Bondage Erotica 2012
Edited by Rachel Kramer Bussel
ISBN 978-1-57344-754-6 $15.95

Best Lesbian Erotica 2014
Edited by Kathleen Warnock
ISBN 978-1-62778-002-5 $15.95

Best Lesbian Erotica 2013
Edited by Kathleen Warnock
Selected and introduced by
Jewelle Gomez
ISBN 978-1-57344-896-3 $15.95

Best Lesbian Erotica 2012
Edited by Kathleen Warnock
Selected and introduced by
Sinclair Sexsmith
ISBN 978-1-57344-752-2 $15.95

Best Gay Erotica 2014
Edited by Larry Duplechan
Selected and introduced by Joe Manetti
ISBN 978-1-62778-001-8 $15.95

Best Gay Erotica 2013
Edited by Richard Labonté
Selected and introduced by Paul Russell
ISBN 978-1-57344-895-6 $15.95

Best Gay Erotica 2012
Edited by Richard Labonté
Selected and introduced by
Larry Duplechan
ISBN 978-1-57344-753-9 $15.95

Best Fetish Erotica
Edited by Cara Bruce
ISBN 978-1-57344-355-5 $15.95

Best Bisexual Women's Erotica
Edited by Cara Bruce
ISBN 978-1-57344-320-3 $15.95

Best Lesbian Bondage Erotica
Edited by Tristan Taormino
ISBN 978-1-57344-287-9 $16.95

Red Hot Erotic Romance

Obsessed
Erotic Romance for Women
Edited by Rachel Kramer Bussel

These stories sizzle with the kind of obsession that is fueled by our deepest desires, the ones that hold couples together, the ones that haunt us and don't let go. Whether just-blooming passions, rekindled sparks or reinvented relationships, these lovers put the object of their obsession first.
ISBN 978-1-57344-718-8 $14.95

Passion
Erotic Romance for Women
Edited by Rachel Kramer Bussel

Love and sex have always been intimately intertwined—and *Passion* shows just how delicious the possibilities are when they mingle in this sensual collection edited by award-winning author Rachel Kramer Bussel.
ISBN 978-1-57344-415-6 $14.95

Girls Who Bite
Lesbian Vampire Erotica
Edited by Delilah Devlin

Bestselling romance writer Delilah Devlin and her contributors add fresh girl-on-girl blood to the pantheon of the paranormal. The stories in *Girls Who Bite* are varied, unexpected, and soul-scorching.
ISBN 978-1-57344-715-7 $14.95

Irresistible
Erotic Romance for Couples
Edited by Rachel Kramer Bussel

This prolific editor has gathered the most popular fantasies and created a sizzling, no-holds-barred collection of explicit encounters in which couples turn their deepest desires into reality.
978-1-57344-762-1 $14.95

Heat Wave
Hot, Hot, Hot Erotica
Edited by Alison Tyler

What could be sexier or more seductive than bare, sun-warmed skin? Bestselling erotica author Alison Tyler gathers explicit stories of summer sex bursting with the sweet eroticism of swimsuits, sprinklers, and ripe strawberries.
ISBN 978-1-57344-710-2 $15.95

* **Free book of equal or lesser value. Shipping and applicable sales tax extra.**
Cleis Press • (800) 780-2279 • orders@cleispress.com
www.cleispress.com

Bestselling Erotica for Couples

Sweet Life
Erotic Fantasies for Couples
Edited by Violet Blue

Your ticket to a front row seat for first-time spankings, breathtaking role-playing scenes, sex parties, women who strap it on and men who love to take it, not to mention threesomes of every combination.
ISBN 978-1-57344-133-9 $14.95

Sweet Life 2
Erotic Fantasies for Couples
Edited by Violet Blue

"This is a we-did-it-you-can-too anthology of real couples playing out their fantasies."
—Lou Paget, author of *365 Days of Sensational Sex*
ISBN 978-1-57344-167-4 $15.95

Sweet Love
Erotic Fantasies for Couples
Edited by Violet Blue

"If you ever get a chance to try out your number-one fantasies in real life—and I assure you, there will be more than one—say yes. It's well worth it. May this book, its adventurous authors, and the daring and satisfied characters be your guiding inspiration."—Violet Blue
ISBN 978-1-57344-381-4 $14.95

Afternoon Delight
Erotica for Couples
Edited by Alison Tyler

"Alison Tyler evokes a world of heady sensuality where fantasies are fearlessly explored and dreams gloriously realized."
—Barbara Pizio, Executive Editor, *Penthouse Variations*
ISBN 978-1-57344-341-8 $14.95

Three-Way
Erotic Stories
Edited by Alison Tyler

"Three means more of everything. Maybe I'm greedy, but when it comes to sex, I like more. More fingers. More tongues. More limbs. More tangling and wrestling on the mattress."
ISBN 978-1-57344-193-3 $15.95

Read the Very Best in Erotica

Fairy Tale Lust
Erotic Fantasies for Women
Edited by Kristina Wright
Foreword by Angela Knight

Award-winning novelist and top erotica writer Kristina Wright goes over the river and through the woods to find the sexiest fairy tales ever written.
ISBN 978-1-57344-397-5 $14.95

In Sleeping Beauty's Bed
Erotic Fairy Tales
By Mitzi Szereto

"Classic fairy tale characters like Rapunzel, Little Red Riding Hood, Cinderella, and Sleeping Beauty, just to name a few, are brought back to life in Mitzi Szereto's delightful collection of erotic fairy tales."
—Nancy Madore, author of *Enchanted: Erotic Bedtime Stories for Women*
ISBN 978-1-57344-376-8 $16.95

Frenzy
60 Stories of Sudden Sex
Edited by Alison Tyler

"Toss out the roses and box of candies. This isn't a prolonged seduction. This is slammed against the wall in an alleyway sex, and it's all that much hotter for it."
—Erotica Readers & Writers Association
ISBN 978-1-57344-331-9 $14.95

Fast Girls
Erotica for Women
Edited by Rachel Kramer Bussel

Fast Girls celebrates the girl with a reputation, the girl who goes all the way, and the girl who doesn't know how to say "no."
ISBN 978-1-57344-384-5 $14.95

Can't Help the Way That I Feel
Sultry Stories of African American Love, Lust and Fantasy
Edited by Lori Bryant-Woolridge

Some temptations are just too tantalizing to ignore in this collection of delicious stories edited by Emmy award-winning and *Essence* bestselling author Lori Bryant-Woolridge.
ISBN 978-1-57344-386-9 $14.95

Fuel Your Fantasies

Carnal Machines
Steampunk Erotica
Edited by D. L. King

In this decadent fusing of technology and romance, outstanding contemporary erotica writers use the enthralling possibilities of the 19th-century steam age to tease and titillate.
ISBN 978-1-57344-654-9 $14.95

The Sweetest Kiss
Ravishing Vampire Erotica
Edited by D. L. King

These sanguine tales give new meaning to the term "dead sexy" and feature beautiful bloodsuckers whose desires go far beyond blood.
ISBN 978-1-57344-371-5 $15.95

The Handsome Prince
Gay Erotic Romance
Edited by Neil Plakcy

A bawdy collection of bedtime stories brimming with classic fairy tale characters, reimagined and recast for any man who has dreamt of the day his prince will come. These sexy stories fuel fantasies and remind us all of the power of true romance.
ISBN 978-1-57344-659-4 $14.95

Daughters of Darkness
Lesbian Vampire Tales
Edited by Pam Keesey

"A tribute to the sexually aggressive woman and her archetypal roles, from nurturing goddess to dangerous predator."—*The Advocate*
ISBN 978-1-57344-233-6 $14.95

Dark Angels
Lesbian Vampire Erotica
Edited by Pam Keesey

Dark Angels collects tales of lesbian vampires, the quintessential bad girls, archetypes of passion and terror. These tales of desire are so sharply erotic you'll swear you've been bitten!
ISBN 978-1-57344-252-7 $13.95

Ordering is easy! Call us toll free or fax us to place your MC/VISA order.
You can also mail the order form below with payment to:
Cleis Press, 2246 Sixth St., Berkeley, CA 94710.

ORDER FORM

QTY	TITLE	PRICE
_____	_____	_____
_____	_____	_____
_____	_____	_____
_____	_____	_____
_____	_____	_____
_____	_____	_____
_____	_____	_____
_____	_____	_____

SUBTOTAL	_____
SHIPPING	_____
SALES TAX	_____
TOTAL	_____

Add $3.95 postage/handling for the first book ordered and $1.00 for each additional
book. Outside North America, please contact us for shipping rates. California residents
add 9% sales tax. Payment in U.S. dollars only.

* Free book of equal or lesser value. Shipping and applicable sales tax extra.

**Cleis Press • Phone: (800) 780-2279 • Fax: (510) 845-8001
orders@cleispress.com • www.cleispress.com
You'll find more great books on our website**

Follow us on Twitter @cleispress • Friend/fan us on Facebook